CAN'T HOLD BACK

RETURNING HOME BOOK 2

SERENA BELL

JELSBA
MEDIA
GROUP

For Robin, Jess, Lindsay, and Janette, my healers. Thank you.

PROLOGUE

"Is this seat taken?"

From her perspective in the grass, he was a giant, with broad shoulders and a luminous smile. She'd always thought it was exaggeration when women said they lost their breath in a man's presence, but she just had.

She got a grip and shook her head. "Pull up some turf." She patted the lawn beside her, and he sat.

He was vivid, like a soldier in a movie: ripped, swaggering, grinning, golden-haired. He'd smiled in her direction earlier, and for a split second she'd thought, *Who me?* before she remembered that she was standing next to Becca. Her sister was a man *magnet*. All the two of them had to do was idle in a patch of sunlight admiring the garden, and sexy six-foot-plus men in butt-hugging jeans and black T-shirts materialized from nowhere—

Abracadabra! Hot guy for Becca.

In the car on the way over here, she'd told Becca that Jake's picnics boasted not just amazing food, but other earthly delights. "We'll get you back on your feet," Alia had promised, sneaking a glance at her sister, slumped in the passenger seat. Ever since Becca's boyfriend had dumped her recently, just as they were getting serious, she rarely smiled.

Becca had been super excited about the guy, and Alia was almost as disappointed as Becca was. She wanted her sister to be happy. Settled. *Cared for.*

Hot Guy for Becca set his plate on the grass. He sat cross-legged, and his thighs and calves, which looked like they'd been hewn from wood, were generously decked with curly golden hair.

"My sister just went to get some food," she told him, pointing.

He cast a glance at Becca, standing by the salad table, loading her plate with potato chips. Tall, beautiful, blond, and *glowing* with vitality.

"You guys don't look anything alike."

"We don't." She forced a smile. It wasn't only blindingly obvious differences, like Becca's blond and Alia's dark hair, but everything else, too—Becca was slim, with hourglass curves, while Alia was "athletic"; Becca had porcelain skin and Alia was generously freckled; Becca's features were classic and even, and Alia was—well, she'd be kind to herself and say "cute."

She sighed.

"Nate Riordan." The man beside her reached out his hand for a shake.

"Alia Drake."

Big hands. Warm. A moment ago, the world had smelled like summer. Like grass gone somewhere to seed, roses in bloom, and the mingled marvels of mesquite smoke and grilling meat.

Now her head was filled with a different scent entirely—soap, shampoo, the faintest whiff of some spicy male deodorant or cologne.

He was going to have no difficulty making Becca forget her romantic troubles. He could probably make any woman blank on her own name.

She retrieved her hand before she could reflect any more on *that.* He was *Becca's* hot guy.

Alia worried about Becca a lot. Probably too much, considering they were now both adults and capable of standing on their own. But it was an old, old habit, born after their father's death and during their mother's long depressions, when Becca had struggled to keep her head—and her self-esteem—above water.

They were both adults now, but Alia totally got what parents meant when they said your worry didn't vanish just because your kid had taken off for college.

"You friends with Mira?" Nate asked, hoisting his burger for a bite.

"Jake. We went to PT school together."

"You're a physical therapist, too, huh? I've always thought that was a cool job."

"I love it. Love the work, love the people."

"Yeah? You're lucky. Not too many people get to say that about their jobs."

"You don't love yours?"

He laughed. "Caught that, did you? I don't have a story like Jake's, all that post-Nine/Eleven conviction. Going to college for me meant a staggering amount of debt, and the only way I could hope to get myself out from under it was to join up. So that's what I did. And it's not that I hate it. I just . . . I guess . . . you find meaning where you can, you know?"

She did, or thought she did, and it made her want to glide straight past small talk and delve in, but instead she asked, "Are you a Ranger, too? Is that how you know Jake?"

"No, actually—Army grunt, between deployments. And I met Jake when he gave a talk. 'A Life of Purpose' or something like that. I was a senior in college, it was career week, and I almost didn't go because I knew I was enlisting, so I figured I knew my purpose, or at least my purpose for a little bit." He gave a wry shake of his gold-streaked head. "But some of my friends were planning to go, and I thought I should at least check it out. And I was, like, okay, here's a guy, a Ranger, out of the Army, missing a leg, doing all this great stuff—competing in triathlons, going back to school, helping other soldiers—"

"Jake's amazing."

"He is," Nate agreed, suddenly serious, and that was almost more dazzling than the smiling version. She found herself sucked into his blue-eyed gaze, a little dazed, nodding. "So fu— freaking inspiring. I mean, not some saint, but a guy who suffered and figured out how to come back stronger, to be a dad and a husband, and how to help tons of people, but also not bragging about it."

She smiled, because, yeah, that was what she loved about Jake, too. Not just the bravery, but: "He won't take any credit for doing what needs to be done."

"Right. Damn, couldn't have said it better. Exactly." He grinned.

Oh, my God, that grin. Confident but not arrogant, his

eyes bright, corners crinkled, a crease that stopped short of being a dimple in one cheek.

She was staring at him, and the moment had stretched too long. *Right.* She looked away and took a hasty bite of potato salad. *Wow.* Really good. Mira's work.

"Now he's building the retreat—have you seen it?"

He shook his head. "Not yet. But he was telling me about it, and it all makes sense. That he'd end up doing that, helping other guys with the transition. He had a tough homecoming."

Jake had come back from Afghanistan with an above-the-knee amputation, having lost both his leg and his teammate to an IED explosion—and promptly discovered he was the father of a seven-year-old he'd had no idea existed.

They exchanged knowing glances, then both turned to watch Jake, who was tossing a football with Sam.

"But he turned it *into* something. And he's made this great life for himself, you know?"

Yeah, again, she knew, but suddenly she couldn't quite get the words to come out around the feeling in her chest. The tightness was caused by thinking about Jake and what he'd lost and found, yes, but it also had something to do with the sympathy, admiration, and longing on Nate's face when he watched father and son together.

"Anyway—" Nate's lopsided smile and half-shrug said, *Back to lighter topics.* "I went up after the talk and said how much I admired what he'd done, and we ended up getting drunk together. So now I'm on the picnic invitation list."

"And once you're on the list, you're on forever. And Jake and Mira know how to throw a party."

They smiled at each other, and he raised his red plastic party cup to hers in a toast. "To the picnic list."

"Hey, guys."

She'd almost forgotten about Becca, who was now standing over them with her plate, looking faintly uncomfortable. As if she were waiting for an invitation she wasn't sure would be extended.

She'd seen that look on her sister's face far too many times. The expression Becca wore after of years of being unsure of herself.

Becca, who hadn't learned to read till she was ten, who called herself dumb way too often, who still found writing almost impossible. Becca, whose boyfriend had told her he needed to be with someone who was his intellectual equal.

Becca, who was Alia's *family*. Because their dad was gone and their mom was—well, she was who she was—and the two of them had still somehow made a childhood out of the muddle.

And *crap*, Alia wasn't supposed to be shopping for a boyfriend for herself. She was supposed to be playing wingman to her sister.

Anyway, Nate really wasn't Alia's type. Alia's life, for better or for worse, had made her into someone who thrived on taking care of people. It didn't tend to work out well for her with guys who were more the fiercely independent alpha types.

And if there was something she knew about Nate Riordan after five minutes in his company, it was that he knew what he wanted and how to get it.

For a split second more, she hesitated, looking between them—the guy who'd just almost made her forget her mission, and her sister, who deserved happiness more than anyone Alia knew.

Then she said, "Nate, Becca. Becca, Nate," and caught Becca's eye and grinned at her sister. *Look what I found for you!*

Nate stood to shake Becca's hand.

See? That right there. The kind of guy for whom chivalry wasn't dead.

He could take care of Becca the way she deserved.

Alia stood, too. Becca was—she was actually smiling at Nate. Or at least most-of-the-way smiling.

God, she'd missed her sister's smile.

Nate smiled back at Becca. Her hand was still in his.

Perfect. The handshake would do its magic, and Becca could handle the rest.

Alia watched the two of them, golden in the sun, and felt—

A curl of something in her chest. The pleasure of a match well made, maybe.

"I'm gonna grab some lemonade. Either of you—"

"No, thanks," Becca said.

"I'm good," Nate said.

Alia walked away.

Half an hour later, Becca caught her arm beside the dessert table.

"Are you *sure*? He talked to you first. You guys looked like you were enjoying yourselves."

When Alia answered, she did it casually, with so much confidence there could be no doubt.

"A hundred percent positive."

She was. A hundred percent positive about wanting to make Becca smile. All the way. All the time.

1

"Come off the foam roller and take a moment to lie on your back," Alia told her class.

Four soldiers slid to their yoga mats in the dim studio.

"How does it feel?"

She held her breath, because she wanted so badly for this class to be a success, and now all she could do was cross her fingers and hope that her best had been good enough.

A few sighs and a moan answered her. The tall redheaded former comm officer said, "Like the floor under my spine is indented."

"That's right," she teased. "While you were on the roller, I went around and dug holes in the floor for all of you."

The sensation was an illusion, created because they'd been resting for so long on their backs on the foam roller, letting their shoulder blades sink toward the floor, opening the muscles along their spines. Now that they were on the floor, their brains were sending them the message that the ground was concave.

They'd all started class today with chips on their shoulders. Three of the four had shown up as a favor to Jake, who ran the R&R veterans' retreat and was Alia's new, temporary boss. The fourth had come willingly but tried to leave once he discovered that they weren't going to be using the Reformer machines, which resembled medieval torture devices more than exercise equipment. All of them had grumbled and sulked, and she'd indulged in a moment of worry that maybe this whole thing had been a bad idea.

Then she'd taken a deep breath, cracked her mental knuckles, and bulled through it. She'd jollied and teased them, leading them through stretching and strengthening and breathing exercises, until the starch had gone out of their attitudes, one by one. Big, tough, ripped men; men who'd shot and killed, fought for their survival, their countries, their buddies; men who were scarred, in chronic pain, struggling to learn to move with prostheses—limp as rags on their mats.

Now, finally, she let herself relax and savor her success—and their comfort. None of them showed the slightest sign of wanting to move, ever.

"Rest as long as you want," she told them. "No one's coming in for another hour. Raise your hand if you want me to bring a blanket to cover you."

They all raised their hands, and her smile broadened. She brought them blankets and covered them. And they let her, like they'd accepted her as Mama Bear.

These were not men who frequently let down their guards, not men who slept well at night—or ever. She'd given them something they needed desperately, and, *God,* she loved that.

She heard a tap on the studio's window and looked up to see Jake.

"I'll be right outside, guys."

She went to the door and slipped out. "Hey."

"You won them over."

She grinned, pleased with herself. "And you said movement therapy would be a tough sell for guys who got a little light exercise by running up mountains with a hundred pounds on their backs."

"I stand corrected."

The admiration was plain in his voice. *Excellent.* Because if she did a good job here during her two-week temporary gig, there was a chance he'd hire her on permanently. And that meant—

That meant not having to go back *there.*

At the thought of her old job, the tension crept back into her neck and shoulders. *Sigh.*

"So, hey," Jake said, more serious. "I screwed up. And I need you to not hate me for it."

Uh-oh.

"I could never hate you," she hazarded.

The hesitation in her voice made them both laugh, but he quickly got serious. "I'm taking off in an hour, but something's . . . come up."

Jake was headed to the airport to take a five-year-anniversary trip to Hawaii with his wife, Mira, which was why he'd asked Alia to come to R&R for two weeks, to fill in for him during his absence.

"I totally forgot you knew him."

"Knew *who*?"

"Mira reminded me. That you guys knew each other."

"Jake, what are you *talking* about?"

She wouldn't yap that way at just any boss, but Jake was a good friend. They'd been at PT school together, not only study and drinking buddies, but also deep admirers of each other's work and perspective, which was why Jake had called her when he'd needed someone to fill in.

"Nate Riordan's here."

All the air went out of her lungs.

"I know it might be weird, since he was with Becca—"

Oh, if only that had been all of it. Nate had indeed dated Becca, and that alone—given that the relationship had ended badly—might have been awkward enough, but Jake didn't know the half of it. Or she hoped he didn't.

Jake sighed. Her wariness must have been all over her face.

"He was discharged—medical—a couple months ago and I tried to get him to come then, but he wasn't having it. He's been living in an apartment in Portland with his cousin, but his cousin met a woman he's serious about, so that's not happening anymore. Basically, all I know is that he had fourth-order blast injuries, moderate traumatic brain injury, some memory loss and cognitive impairment at first, but big improvements on that front. But it sounds like he also has some mystery pain. He's been back a couple months and he's been taking a lot of painkillers, but he quit a few days ago—"

"Cold turkey?"

"Just un-cold-turkey enough not to kill himself, I think," Jake said. "He's in pretty bad shape now. Out of the worst of it, but you know what that's like."

She did. There was no worse pain than the pain unmasked when an opiate haze lifted.

"Why'd he do that? Quit taking the pills?" She couldn't judge, without seeing and talking to him, whether quitting painkillers was the right choice for him, but going nearly cold turkey was brutal.

"All he told me is he has something important to do and he needs to be clearheaded. You'll have to ask him. He wasn't very forthcoming about anything. He mainly said he needed a place to go, and wanted to know if my offer of him coming here was still open. I said, 'Hell, yeah.' And then Mira reminded me about his history with Becca. So, look, if it's going to be too weird, we can figure something out."

She did *not* want to tell Jake she couldn't hack this. He was supposed to be on an airplane in an hour, and she was supposed to be the woman who could handle anything that came up while he was gone. In their phone conversation, when he'd called to ask if she could fill in for him, he'd made it clear that he thought the toughest part of the job was the emotional burden of dealing with psychically and physically injured soldiers. She had to show him she had enough strength and perspective to do this. She couldn't afford to be high-maintenance now over some guy her sister had dated. Even if—

Even if he wasn't just *some guy her sister had dated.*

But for all intents and purposes, that was all he'd been. Right?

And she did *not* want to go back to Elijah Bay Rehab.

The day before Jake's call had been a pretty typical day at Elijah Bay. Her last appointment of the day had been with seventy-two-year-old Mrs. Stenno, who'd arrived buoyant. She'd washed her own hair that morning for the first time since the stroke, and had gotten it squeaky clean. Her daughter had declared her capable of taking care of herself and was planning to move back home.

I get my house back, she'd said giddily.

Alia lived for those moments.

But then, after Alia ushered Mrs. Stenno out, her supervisor had called her into his office, in his ironside battleship voice.

"This isn't a yoga retreat, Alia. Chris Price says you were using some kind of tapping technique on Mrs. Stenno? And when I had to take Elisabeth Toole for you last week, she wanted to do 'the visualization stuff I do with Alia.' You're wasting patient time. You're wasting *my* time."

She took a deep breath. "I'm getting results."

She had proof, and not just anecdotal proof. She had better recovery times than the other PTs. She had better recovery times than her supervisor.

And that, she knew, was at the heart of this.

"I've told you before how I feel about the earthy-crunchy-granola stuff."

This wasn't the first time he'd confronted her, and her pent-up frustration threatened to break from its bonds. She made herself take a few deep breaths. "Tapping and visualization aren't earthy-crunchy. They're pain-management best practices."

"You don't decide what's best practices at Elijah Bay," her supervisor said darkly. "*I* decide what's best practices at Elijah Bay. And if I hear anything else about this kind of bullshit, you can find yourself another job."

She made up her mind then that she would. But it had to be a certain *kind* of opportunity. Because physical therapy wasn't just a job for her. Relieving other people's pain, helping them to live full, active lives despite setbacks or permanent disabilities—it was her passion. And she wanted to do it in a setting where she could really make a difference.

That was why she'd been so thrilled the next day when Jake had called her with the temporary offer. R&R was the perfect opportunity.

Some women her age—twenty-six—might not love the idea of going to live in the woods in the middle of nowhere. Not exactly the best place to build a social life or meet a mate. But Alia was different. She knew she didn't need romance to be happy. Friendship, yes; human love and kindness and companionship, yes—all of which she had in spades from her Seattle buddies and her amazing sister—but romantic love, not so much. It had a way of going awry for her, leaving her out in the cold. She wanted to walk a different path, a path of service and purpose. She wanted to be where she was needed.

She wanted to give something back to these men who had given so much themselves.

So, yeah, no way she was going to refuse to help Nate, regardless of history. She was a professional, a big girl with a mission that didn't include fussing over an old crush. If the cost of working for Jake at R&R was that she had to be in close quarters with Nate, she could handle that. Besides, she owed Nate. If she could give him some peace, some relief, maybe it would help compensate for—for what she'd done.

"Of course I'll work with him. The thing with Becca isn't an issue."

That for sure was a lie wrapped in the truth. Nate's relationship with Becca might have been short-lived—maybe even doomed from the start—but there was nothing small or simple about the tangle Alia had managed to make of it.

Jake exhaled deeply, and Alia realized he'd been prepared for her to say no. "Well, good. I'll run past Sibby's desk and schedule Nate in today or tomorrow. Can't imagine anyone I'd trust more with his well-being. And can't imagine any hands I'd feel more comfortable leaving my patients in. This means a lot to me *and* to Mira."

She shoved him lightly. "Go on. Get out of here. Enjoy your trip. Don't give any of this another thought."

He saluted her, turned sharply on one foot, and marched off. She laughed.

But she wasn't laughing as she turned back toward the studio, where her relaxed soldiers were snoring in stereo.

I hope your trust in me is justified, Jake.

Because she'd been a fool more than once before, where Nate Riordan was concerned.

2

N ate lifted a kayak off the rack, and a spasm of pain in his shoulder caught him off guard. The kayak tilted, and he righted it quickly and lowered it to the ground. Cracking the resort's kayak wouldn't be a good way to return the favor Jake had done by taking him in.

He was damn grateful to Jake. For inviting him to stay at R&R, and for keeping the offer open even after Nate had stubbornly refused it the first time. And he was grateful to Braden and his grandparents, for giving him a project. A reason to get clean and stay that way, something to hold on to as he'd flushed the last oxys down the toilet. A purpose to cling to as he'd picked up the phone and dialed Jake's number and on the long drive down from Seattle, when the pain in his head and neck had filled his mind and almost drowned out the Mariners game on the radio.

But somehow he'd kept his eyes on the road and his foot on the gas.

I got this, J.J.

He rubbed his shoulder, shrugged it a few times, but that

only made things worse. He was going to have to bull through it today. And tomorrow. And the next day.

He crossed to the shed for a life jacket and a paddle.

The pain was mysterious and ever-changing. Sometimes it was a stab behind his eyes or a wave of nausea, the migraines he'd been told to expect in a wake of the blast. More frequently, it was his neck, his shoulders, his back, all of which had taken a beating when the blast had thrown him. That made sense. But sometimes the pain obeyed no logic. It started in one place and spread, lighting up points all over his body until he felt patched together out of signal flares of pain. *Here!* And *Here!* And *Here again!* Or it was everywhere at once, like the flu, an ache that told him where he began and the rest of the world ended.

It had definitely been worse since he'd watched his pain meds spin in the water funnel.

He'd seriously contemplated snatching them back up. He knew what that meant. You only thought about putting your hands in the toilet to recover melting tablets if you were an addict. And of course he'd known, long before he'd flushed, that he was. But there was nothing like having it spelled out. *This drug owns you.*

This pain owns you.

But he didn't care about that right now. He was going to do this, keep moving forward, haul himself bodily over every obstacle, and cling to the incline with bleeding fingertips if necessary.

With effort, he slid the kayak to the edge of the dock and into the water. He wedged his paddle behind the seat and slipped in. He'd kayaked a ton as a kid, so he knew the ropes, including self-rescue. Still, he'd forgotten the particular gravity of a slim boat like this one, and as he pushed off, he almost capsized. The effort of stabilizing sent arrows of pain up the right side of his back. *Damn.*

"Nate."

There was a woman standing on the dock.

Alia Drake.

"We had an appointment." She frowned across the small but growing span of water between them, her arms crossed.

He didn't bother asking how she'd known to look for him here. When he'd headed this way, he'd walked past a group of guys sitting on the back porch. If she was hunting for him, she would have asked them if they'd seen him.

"Sorry," he muttered. Only he wasn't. He'd deliberately blown off the appointment, because—well, for a lot of reasons. Because he'd had enough physical therapy to be sure that whatever was wrong with him, PT wasn't going to fix it. Because he hated medical offices and doctors and nurses and PTs. And most of all, because the last thing he needed right now was Alia Drake.

The space between them was widening. The temptation to start paddling full speed away from her was strong, and the only thing that kept him from doing it was the fact that pain still had his neck in a death grip. He took a deep breath and waited for it to subside.

She turned away from him, and for a moment he thought she'd given up, but then she came toward him with a life-jacket and paddle in her hands. He watched as she lifted a kayak from the rack and dropped it effortlessly into the water.

Fuck.

She slid neatly in, surprisingly graceful for such a tall woman, and pushed off.

"I don't want company."

"Tough. I told Jake I'd help you."

"And this is helping me how?" He was mad enough to look her full in the face, and that was a big mistake.

She looked right back at him, utterly uncowed, and her gray-green eyes were generously fringed with sooty lashes. Her cheeks were pink with anger.

She was startlingly pretty. He'd privately thought her the more beautiful of the two sisters, even though Becca's beauty was more conventional. When Alia had made it clear that she wasn't interested—that her sister was the available one— Nate had given only one backward, regretful glance— metaphorically—before turning his appreciation on Becca.

But now he admired the thick, glossy strands of Alia's straight, medium-length dark hair. She wore no makeup, and he was charmed—against his will—by the freckles scattered over her nose and cheekbones. She was tall for a woman, and strong. On the dock, when her legs had been level with his eyes, he'd surprised himself with the impulse to run his hands over the muscle in her legging-clad thighs and strong bare calves. And yet—he'd noted, before the life jacket and spray skirt had covered most of her—she had curves, too. Nothing showy. Everything in proportion. She looked—real. That was it. As if she were built for *purpose,* not for any man's entertainment.

Especially not his.

"Why didn't you come to your appointment?"

"Because I don't need PT." He turned his boat and paddled out toward the center of the lake.

She pulled alongside him and kept pace. Every stroke sent pain shooting up the back of his neck.

"You're hurting."

It was a statement, not a question.

"I can see it on your face. The way you're holding your upper body."

"It's not that bad."

That was a lie, and this was making it worse. The kayak, the paddling, Alia's scrutiny, fierce on his face.

He wasn't going to do Suzy and Jim and Braden any good if he couldn't even paddle into the middle of a goddamn lake.

He wanted to howl his frustration to the sky, but Alia was there, watching him, and he couldn't.

"Jake said you were taking oxycodone, and then you quit. Why'd you do that?"

He had to admire her style—not giving him a chance to deny the assertion before she threw the question at him— and the way she was barely breathless from the effort of paddling. She was *tough,* one of the things he remembered liking about her. If there was a person on earth who would understand why he had flushed those pills down the toilet, it was her. "I felt like they were the boss of me, not the other way around."

She nodded.

"I need to take a kid on a kayaking trip in three weeks. Can't be popping pills the whole time."

"But this is okay? You think the kid's not going to notice that you're in pain?"

Her meaning was harsh, but her voice was kind. Firm. Not a challenge so much as a real question.

Their paddles dipped into the water. They had quietly come into synchrony, skimming over the water alongside each other, nearly silent.

"Most people don't notice."

But she'd seen it right away. In his face, she said. In the way he held his upper body.

He remembered that she was a good observer. She'd seen him, seen through him, as early as their first meeting at the picnic. Later, she'd written about the world so clearly in her emails and letters—though of course back then he'd thought they were Becca's.

"Why is it so important to go on this kayaking trip?"

They were almost across the lake now. The flat expanse of gray-blue water was surrounded by forest. The only civilization visible was the retreat itself, where he could see people moving around, as small and busy as insects. He wished he hadn't come out here. He'd hated the idea of her office, but this was worse, the two of them out here and her question dangling, as if she had a right to know the answer.

He chose a partial truth. "The kid, Braden. I served with his dad. He's . . . gone. He and Braden were supposed to do a kayaking trip this summer."

"I'm sorry," she said quietly.

Strange how easily voices carried out here, how you could hear a whisper spoken several feet away.

"Yeah, well."

"Let me help you."

The pain carved a channel down his back, as if in protest of all the times people had said that to him. All the times it had given him hope, and all the times that hope had turned out to be false. The pain got under his ribs, the way it so often did, and made him mean.

"Like you helped Becca?"

———

3

A lia filled her plate with vegetable lasagna and
made her way through the chaos and hubbub in
the retreat's big dining room.

She liked the style of the room, a mash-up of ski-lodge
chic and French restaurant—bare wooden tables, squat
candles, Fiestaware, and dim lighting. She wondered
whether Jake or Mira had made the design decisions. She
could see it playing out either way.

"So? How's it going?" Gabi demanded, as Alia sat with two
of her new friends. The retreat's activities director, Gabi was
sweetly chubby, dark-haired, dark-skinned, and thirtysome-
thing. On Alia's first night, she'd grabbed Alia's arm and
urged her to come sit with her. "With only a few women on
staff, we all keep an eye out for one another," she'd explained.

Alia took a bite of the lasagna. All the food at the resort so
far had been amazing—healthy *and* hearty—and this was no
exception. "I think it's going pretty well."

"The residents like you," Melinda said. Melinda taught
paddleboarding, kayaking, canoeing, waterskiing—pretty

much anything that involved a boat. "You're getting rave reviews. And off-color comments. About, you know, happy endings."

Alia blushed. "Um, yuck."

"Just ignore it." Melinda tucked a bit of curly hair behind her ear. She was married to Joe, who ran the retreat's stables, but he was off leading a sunset horseback ride.

"It's the downside of being one of just a few women in a testosterone bath." Gabi smiled wryly. "And somehow it got out that you're single, too. I'll say that's one good thing about Geoff. Keeps the horny horde at bay." She wrinkled her nose. "If he were better at his stud work, I might not mind so much."

Already Alia knew about Gabi that her husband was fifteen years older, a heavy drinker, and sexually neglectful. Actually, she'd learned that in her first fifteen minutes of association with Gabi, along with a bunch of additional facts about both Gabi and other staff members.

A scrap of deep voice caught her attention. Nate was sitting not far away, with a bunch of guys, chatting amiably. *Huh.* But she guessed it made sense. He didn't hate the world, only *her*—and she had to admit he had good reason.

Like you helped Becca?

She hadn't tried to apologize or explain her past behavior. Instead, she'd paddled away from him, because she'd known she was too defensive to continue the conversation. But she hadn't given up on the idea of helping him with his pain. Far from making her feel like she shouldn't interfere, his accusatory tone on the lake had reminded her how much she owed him. *I could make up for what I did. I could give him something back in exchange for what I took away.*

He looked like hell. Gray-faced, hollow-eyed, scruffy, like he hadn't seen a razor in days. It had been two years since she'd seen him, but he could have been ten years older. And he'd lost weight. Before, he'd been built like a running back, packed solid into T-shirts and jeans that were loose now.

He'd been golden, irresistible, one hundred percent confident.

But that was all history. Nate's vitality, his dazzle, how Alia had given him, like a twisted gift, to Becca. And how that had come back to haunt all three of them.

Right now, he was just a guy who hurt. Who needed help. She could totally handle that. She'd figure out a way to get him in her office, on her table. She'd get him talking, track the pain to its source, root it out.

"Earth to Alia!"

"Ah. Just trying to figure out a work problem. Sorry, I'm here. You were saying. Husbands protect you from the hordes."

"At least Joe provides some services above and beyond security," Gabi said to Melinda, with the expressive equivalent of a wink-wink, nudge-nudge.

"Joe does earn his keep," said Melinda, contentedly.

Alia grinned.

"So, no one special in your life?"

Both women leaned in, eyes gleaming.

"No. Last boyfriend was about six months ago, and I'm actually enjoying the dry spell."

"Is there a story to go with Mr. Last Boyfriend?"

"Peter." She told the story, such as it was. Peter had been in a bad place when she met him, unemployed and more or less homeless, which had propelled their relationship into high gear.

He'd moved in with her quickly and had loads of time to devote to wooing her, and for a brief period of time she'd thought he was *the one.* But around the nine-month mark, when she'd been sure he was about to put a ring on her finger, he'd gotten a job and she'd discovered that he was a workaholic. So when he'd suggested he move into his own apartment, she hadn't minded as much as she should have. And then things, well, faded away.

"So you liked him better when he was a sad sack."

"Yeah." She smiled. "Kinda."

"Take my word for it, though, sad sack is *not* a good long-term proposition." Gabi sighed again.

A few tables away, Nate lowered a forkful of food that was halfway to his mouth, his face lined with pain. She could see it clearly even from here, with her well-developed radar.

The guy next to Nate leaned over. She filled in the dialogue: *Hey, man, you okay?*

Nate shook him off. *Fine.*

You don't look fine.

Alia worried that even though this was a drug-free, alcohol-free retreat, it was impossible to keep stuff from filtering in. A guy who'd given up oxy cold turkey would almost assuredly be offered that or a substitute once his friends knew he was suffering. And off prescription, no longer parceling out the tablets under someone else's watchful eyes . . . that was when the real trouble started.

Nate was getting up now, waving his hand to assure his table mates it was nothing. *Just hitting the latrine,* she imagined him saying. But she saw it behind his eyes, written in the creases in his forehead, the deepening lines at the corners of his features: It wasn't nothing.

Before she could think it through, she was on her feet, pushing her chair back. "Hey, guys? I have to try to convince someone they need PT, okay? I'll be right back."

"Ha!" said Gabi. "You have an even tougher job than I do. I just have to convince guys they want to watch action movies and play flag football."

Alia made a face at her and went after Nate.

He wasn't in the hallway outside the dining room. She hesitated, then headed for the stairs.

She'd looked up his room number when he'd failed to show up for his appointment, tracking him there unsuccessfully before she thought to ask the guys on the back porch whether they'd seen him.

Just before the staircase, she heard a low, short groan of pain—more of a grunt, really. Not quite human. A wounded animal. She turned back. She'd almost missed him.

He'd ducked into an alcove, the doorway of one of the first-floor meeting rooms. He was pressed into the corner, one arm up above his head as if to brace himself.

"Nate."

"Go away."

"Nate, please let me help you."

He raised his face and his eyes glittered. "What, witnessing my humiliation once wasn't enough for you?"

She reached out a hand, but he flung his arm out and knocked hers away. "Get out of here."

"Give me a chance. One chance. If I can't help, I promise I'll leave you alone."

"No."

She couldn't make him accept her help. He'd made his

position more than clear. She turned to go. Then a thought struck her.

"For Braden," she said, turning back again. "If you won't let me help you for *you*, do it for Braden."

A long moment passed. The only sound was his breath, hard and ragged. Then he looked up, defeat in his eyes. And nodded.

SITTING IN THE RECEPTION AREA, waiting for Alia to call him into her office, he repeated "for Braden" over and over like a mantra, because this *sucked*. He would have been perfectly happy to have never laid eyes on Alia or Becca again as long as he lived, but because the universe had a savage sense of humor, Jake had gone on vacation and left Alia in charge of pain relief.

She's the best, Jake had said. *I hate to say it, but she's better than me. If there's any way to make the pain stop, short of numbing yourself to death, she will find it.*

He didn't believe it. But she'd said the magic words, *For Braden,* and she'd made him a deal he couldn't resist: If she couldn't help him, she'd leave him alone.

Plus, last night he had hurt so ferociously, he'd been ready to beg, borrow, or steal pills. And he didn't want to even flirt with that thought.

When she'd said she would help him, he'd briefly thought she'd meant right then. Right there. That she would lay hands on and somehow transform the pain, and him. But of course it made sense that she was just asking him to schedule an appointment, like anyone else. Any physical therapist would have certain professional boundaries, and that probably went double for a woman working among so many alpha men, and triple for working in a setting where the pain never stopped and you were geographically available 24/7.

"Nate."

She always said his name like it was a statement of fact. A conclusion.

He raised his head from where he'd rested it in his hands and regarded the woman standing before him.

Not head-turning. Not flamboyantly pretty. But her eyes were warm and her hair shone in the sunlight, and her gray T-shirt hugged her curves, and if the situation hadn't sucked so bad, if he hadn't still been pissed at both her and her sister, if he didn't feel like he'd been run over by a tank, he might have felt a stirring of lust.

That would have been the final straw, so it was damn good it wasn't the case.

He got to his feet, unsteady. A week since the oxy had gone down the toilet, and still not quite clean. He could feel the hunger in his veins, clamoring at him. He felt dirty and corrupted and, God, *dizzy*. He prayed he wouldn't throw up in her office.

"Follow me."

He did. She wore a short sporty skirt over her leggings, and if he'd had a shred of energy to give a shit, he would have said she had a nice ass.

He didn't remember Alia having a nice ass. Becca, yes. He didn't remember a thing about Alia's ass, actually, which was probably because he'd schooled himself not to look at it. He wasn't the kind of guy who shopped around when he was dating someone, and Becca had been plenty beautiful enough to hold his attention, once she'd snared it.

"You can sit there." She gestured at a chair and climbed onto a stool beside a computer on a cart. "So. You have some pain."

He couldn't decide if he was pissed that she was going to pretend that they were any therapist-patient pair or grateful that she wasn't going to make him deconstruct the past. Grateful, he decided. He didn't have the energy for rehashing anything. There was now, and pain, and *fuck,* he hoped Jake was right and she knew what she was doing.

"It's not that bad."

She made a face, as if to say *We both know that isn't true.* "Tell me about the pain."

"Mostly my back. Spine and right side. And it goes up into my neck. And shoulder. And then sometimes into my arm and hand. And I get headaches, too."

She asked him more questions. Could he point to where it hurt on his back? How would he characterize the pain? Was it always the same place in his arm and hand? He did his best to answer. He told her about how it was always different, that it seemed to thrive on blindsiding him. That it didn't follow rules.

"Jake said it was a quaternary blast injury. You've heard that term before, right? Fourth-order—"

"Yeah, I know."

"Your kind of pain—chronic, unpredictable—is pretty common with that type of injury. We don't understand as well as we should exactly what effect percussion has on all the tissues of the body."

He nodded. "They compared it to shaken baby syndrome."

She nodded. "Haven't heard that one, but it makes sense. We don't know what happens to human tissue when you traumatize it all over. We do know the brain doesn't like being shaken." She frowned. "Let's see what your range of motion looks like. Stand up."

She made him turn his head. Tilt from side to side. Swivel at the waist. Reach forward, reach backward. Step, step back.

"Tell me when it hurts."

"Everything hurts."

She frowned. "Tell me when it hurts more."

He tried, but his "nows" didn't match her actions. The pain wasn't following her lead. It had its own logic.

He hated the pain the way you could only hate something living. The way you'd hate a nemesis.

She made a humming sound in the back of her throat, pressed her lips together. "I want to test your strength."

She made him squeeze a grip with foam handles and a thick spring in the middle, then put his arms out and fight her while she pushed down, back, up, forward. She told him to extend a leg and resist as she tried to force it back down.

As she worked, her hair shaded her face from his view. She kept her body at a distance from his, even when she manipulated his limbs. Not enough of a distance, though, that he could ignore her perky breasts at eye level, the hint of nipple poking through her T-shirt, that sweet and generous curve from waist to hip.

Her hands on his arms and legs were professional, competent, but that didn't stop him from noticing the quality of her touch. Warm fingers. Firm, prodding but not poking, holding but not gripping. A point of not-quite-pleasure in the middle of the pain.

It had been a long time since anyone had touched him. The last time had probably been at the VA hospital, the culmination of a long line of doctors' visits that had yielded diagnoses and prognoses and regimens, but no relief.

She nodded, as if affirming something to herself. "No obvious weakness. That's good. Sit."

He did.

"Can you tell me about the blast?"

He shrugged. "If I have to."

"Sometimes it's helpful. I ask people who've been in car accidents or had other traumatic injuries, too. Sometimes there's a detail that helps things make more sense. Does this hurt?" She touched his neck on both sides.

He nodded.

"And this?" She reached under and dug her fingers in at the base of his skull.

He almost jumped off the table.

"I'll take that as a yes. Here?" Under his collarbone.

Not as bad, but enough to make him flinch. "Yeah."

"Here?"

She picked out points on his body one by one. *Yes, yes, and yes.*

She crossed the room and got a tennis ball. She began to tap it on his neck, his shoulders, his chest, his arms. Down to his hands. It was a strange but not unpleasant sensation. So was the brush of her breath over his skin as she leaned near.

"What are you doing?"

"Tapping is a way of telling the muscles that it's okay to let go. One of the things that happens with chronic pain is that you tighten around it. You protect the pain, effectively. It can create a feedback loop, where the tightening is causing more pain than the original injury."

The tapping was soothing. Like rain on the roof. He hadn't slept in weeks. Months. Years, maybe. He was going to fall asleep sitting up. He hoped he wouldn't snore. Or wake up screaming from a nightmare and trying to strangle her, like vets always did on primetime TV.

"So. The blast."

He sighed, resigning himself. "The guard tower was hit. I was at the base of the tower—Fuck," he said, because the pain had doubled down. "Oh, fuck, that hurts. Stop. Stop it! You hit something bad. You're not helping."

She was quiet for a moment, her hands still, the ball suspended over his right shoulder.

Then she said, "Lie down."

"That's not going to help. Nothing helps when it gets like this."

"Lie down." Her voice was soft, but there was iron in it.

It was hard to obey, because the pain twisted, like someone had gotten his hands inside Nate's body and was wringing him along his spine, trying to snap him. He clenched teeth. Fists. He lowered himself gingerly to an elbow, then lay flat out on the bed.

Mother of God, make it stop.

4

———

You didn't have to be a pain-management guru to see it. It wasn't the tapping that had hurt him. It was talking about what had happened. It was remembering.

The tender points on his body told her that his brain was overreacting to pain signals. He was feeling more pain than there was, like a mic and speakers in a terrible feedback loop. It was pretty common with trauma, particularly trauma that had both a physiological and a psychological component.

The first step was breaking the loop.

She put her hands on his shoulders.

His skin, even through his T-shirt, was much warmer than she was expecting, and the sensation surged through her fingers with a shock that she'd failed to brace herself for. That sheer, electric human connection.

If a physical therapist has natural feelings of attraction toward a patient, he/she must sublimate those feelings in order to avoid sexual exploitation of the patient.

Words to that effect had been all over her ethics textbook.

She pulled her hands away for a moment. Recalibrated her mind. Put her hands back on his skin. The sensation was less intense this time, but still there. Like the heat in his body threw a switch beneath her surface.

Sublimate.

She knew what it meant, but she really wasn't sure how the hell one *accomplished* it. She'd never thought to ask.

Maybe this was a bad idea. She'd thought of it as making reparations, but it was starting to look more like making the same mistake twice.

It wasn't like she had a lot of choices here. She had a man in pain on her table. He'd been treating his pain with an addictive painkiller. She was currently the only physical therapist on staff. A litany of facts that didn't give a shit about her feelings, natural or unnatural.

Surely treating him—despite any stray "natural feelings of attraction"—was a lesser evil than kicking him out of her office and probably sending him back to the pill bottle. Especially since she'd already screwed up his life once because she couldn't control her attraction to him.

A physical therapist stands in a relationship of trust to each patient and has an ethical obligation to act in the patient's best interest and to avoid any exploitation or abuse of the patient.

Noticing that her body reacted chemically to the nearness of his wasn't exploitation or abuse. And it was pretty clear that it was in Nate's best interest right now to break the pain loop.

Tentatively, she sent heat into her own fingers, warmed the area over his collarbone. So much tension vibrating in him. Maybe that was all she was feeling, the live-wire coiled energy of a man who'd been wound too tight. She was used to all kinds of electricity pouring off people, the accumulated impulses that a human body stored and shed. What she'd felt a moment ago was just that, another form of strange energy. Nothing to make herself crazy over.

She felt more confident now. *Right.* Nate was in pain. She could help.

She pressed his shoulders gently down, trying to give his neck a little more room. She kneaded with her thumbs, urging the thick knot of muscle to let go. A firm, businesslike touch. Professional strokes.

God, his skin is smooth.

She watched as his lips, which had been pressed together, softened. Loosened, relaxed. Felt something uncoil in her own body. In her chest. Lower.

Damn it.

Sublimate.

The PT ethics hadn't said she couldn't *feel* natural attraction. It just said she couldn't act on it. She wasn't acting on it. She was feeling it and going about her work and her business regardless of it.

She rested her hands where they'd started, on his upper chest. Her fingertips skirted the swell of his pecs. Even depleted, fatigued, stripped of whatever had once made him glow, Nate had a nice chest.

Not relevant.

Maybe she needed a focal point. Something that mattered more than the smoothness of Nate's skin at the base of his neck. Something that mattered more than the pulse beating in the hollow below his throat. Something that mattered more than the sharp smell of soap, the faint, clean scent of deodorant, and the salt-musk combo that was Nate himself.

R&R. The job.

Right. The job.

She shook it off—the chemical buzz of his flesh under her hands, that pulse point throbbing with life, how much she wanted to bury her nose in his hair, at the crook of his neck, where dark hair made a rough pattern under his T-shirt. To see where the scents concentrated strongest.

It's one-sided, she reminded herself. *He doesn't feel it. He's not lying there thinking about what I smell like, or if he is, he's wishing I'd had a breath mint or had worn better antiperspirant. Or he's still pissed at me because of what happened with Becca.*

There was no buzz. No pulse. No tsunami of scents. Not in Nate's mind.

There never was, and there never will be, because he's never, ever been attracted to you. The attraction was all in your own head.

There, she thought, with satisfaction. That *works.*

Nothing like a little humiliation to drown those natural feelings of attraction.

THERE WAS pain inside of pain, pain unfolding out of pain, and then there was the heat of her hands. Something let go in his chest with a ping, and all the tension he'd been holding in his shoulders slid free. *Holy fuck.* Then there was stillness, peace, unfolding out of pain, his brain confused by the suddenness of it all.

There was still pain, but it was quieter now. Like surf roaring behind double-paned glass. Not wrenching anymore, but like something trying to argue its way to the surface of his mind.

And her hands on his shoulders. Smoothing over the bare skin of his neck and along the fabric of his shirt as it rode his collarbone. As if she were brushing something off him.

She guided his head to one side, exposing bare neck. He wanted to tilt his head back, to hide that vulnerable artery, but her grip was firm, and he made himself lie still against rising panic, and in a moment the touch of her fingertips, probing at tight muscle, made him forget fear.

Oh, God, don't stop.

The thought came from nowhere.

I want you to hold the weight of my head, just like this, from now on. So I don't have to. So I can let go like this.

He'd had no idea how heavy his head was. What an effort it was to hold it up. How good it would feel to give someone else the job.

"You're hired." His voice came out fainter than he'd expected, husky, like he'd just woken up.

"To be your physical therapist?"

"To hold my head."

"You like that?"

She was evidently amused. She set his head down and picked up an arm instead. "If you like that, you'll love this." She hefted it. "Go limp. No, really limp. Let go." She shook his arm for emphasis.

He couldn't, though.

"I'm holding you. Let go."

He did, with a rush of relief and pleasure that swelled hard in his gut. She had all the weight of his arm supported by hers, and she was lifting and twisting and tugging in a way that made him realize how tightly he'd been holding himself together.

She did the other arm, then went to the foot of the table. Her hand on his ankle was the whole world. Warm, the fingers pressing into spots he hadn't known were filled with pain. That hollow on either side of the heel—that had been pain. The arch of his foot—that had been pain. She did the other foot, the same way.

She tugged gently on his legs so he rocked on the table, and, *God, that*. That was bliss.

She came back to his neck, found a muscle he hadn't known he had. She followed it to his jaw, down into his shoulder. Behind his shoulder blade. She wasn't digging in. She was just stroking, defining. His mind followed the stroke. It was hypnotic. Rhythmic.

Her fingers found a spot under his arm and teased space into it where there had been none.

The pain receded further and further, like something being pulled out on the tide. Like the sweet, thick warmth of the painkillers, except it was only the pain that was being pulled under, not his mind. His mind had fallen open, empty. Before she started, he'd been made up of pain, and now he was lava.

And then he thought, *But it won't last*. Because he'd had massages once or twice before and they helped, but the relief didn't stick. The chiro hadn't stuck, either. Nor the acupuncture. The pain always came back, sometimes worse than before, as if it were vengeful.

"Shh. What are you thinking about?"

She'd somehow read his thoughts in his body, and sure enough, the lava was gone and he'd gotten colder. The muscles she'd coaxed open tugged back toward their old postures.

"You got tense again."

"It doesn't work. It doesn't last. All this stuff—the pain goes away for a little bit, but it's always back. That's why I started taking the pills. Because at least they were something I could count on. They worked the same every time."

"We'll get you there." She sounded supremely confident. "The important thing is, we got you out of that loop. And we'll get you out of the next one—"

"But what if you can't—"

"We *will*. And we'll learn more about how to get you out, more and more, so you'll be able to do it yourself eventually. And then you won't need pills and you won't need me. That's my goal. To make you not need me. That's always my goal as a physical therapist."

"I can't imagine that now."

"It will happen. I promise. You have to trust me." She slid her fingers under his head, hooking them under the edge of his skull, exerting gentle traction. "Like this. Like you trust me to hold your head."

He lay still for a moment, soaking up the feeling of not being responsible for that particular weight. Then he said, "It's like someone stabbed something in your eardrums."

"That's how the pain feels?"

"No. The blast. Like being pounded and shaken and rung like a bell. I was thrown, and I lost consciousness. And then I opened my eyes and there was nothing there. No tower. Just —sky."

"Jesus."

"And—"

"Braden's dad. J.J. He was gone, too."

If she flinched, he didn't feel the vibrations of it against his skull. She exhaled softly.

He would trust her because he had to, because she was the next step forward.

He gave her the weight of his head, gave himself over to her. The pleasure of giving in was still there, even though the pain was skulking around the edges of his world again.

It was only much later, lying on the narrow extra-long twin bed in the room Jake had set aside for him, that he remembered. Who she was. That she'd deceived him once before. That she wasn't someone he could trust.

5

S he was wiping down the table after her 9 a.m. patient when Sibby, Jake's receptionist and assistant, poked her head into the office.

"You have a walk-in."

Sibby, who could have been anywhere between fifty and seventy, generically grandmotherly, had her arms crossed, and she sounded pissed. It didn't bother Alia. Sibby always got pissed when people didn't have appointments. Alia loved Sibby, for the easy way she managed the front desk, turning impatient veterans into well-behaved little boys with a stern glance.

"Send him in." Alia tossed the towel in the wash and set the disinfectant on the counter. She'd been planning to spend the hour replying to emails, but she was just as happy to take care of someone who needed it. She straightened her row of pain-management reference books and tried to use one of them to make the rest stand up.

A voice behind her said, "The woman at the desk said you could see me now."

The little hairs on the back of her neck stood up. She didn't have to turn around.

"Hi, Nate." She kept her voice professional but not too friendly. God, she wished he wasn't here. She wished she could just send him away, tell him that Sibby had made a mistake and she couldn't see a patient right now after all.

"Pain's back. You said you'd make it go away."

She'd been hoping not to see him for several days. He'd made another appointment for four days out, and Jake would be back in a week and a half, which meant she could probably get away with seeing Nate only twice more. Then Jake would come back and take over, and the question of exactly how one sublimated natural feelings of attraction—and guilty shame—would be moot.

In the meantime, she'd promised herself, she'd keep things strictly on the up-and-up. She'd schedule only mid-morning visits, she'd keep the door cracked or open, and she'd devote a minimal amount of the appointment to hands-on work, leaving more time for stretching and strengthening and reprogramming his pain response.

So much for the best laid plans. Of course the best laid plans had never included brain-melting chemistry or an unprofessional desire to take advantage of his prostrate form.

But she couldn't tell him about either of those things.

There was no one else to refer him to. And he was clearly in pain again. When she finally turned to him, she could see it right away. His hands were squeezed into fists at his sides. Last night, he'd looked so young with the pain smoothed off his face. Young and—free, almost, a look something like the abandon of giving in to sleep. But he'd stayed awake on the table, his breaths lengthening and sometimes slipping into sighs—of relief or maybe pleasure, she wasn't sure—and she didn't let herself think too hard about it. If the chemical effect of touching his bare skin had floored her, the sound of those sighs had nearly knocked her out of her shoes.

"I—" She was readying excuses. If she could put him off now, if she could keep visits to the minimum she'd imagined —she'd be—

Safe, she was thinking. But safe from what? He had no designs on her. Never had. And it wasn't like she was going to lose control and attack him. Nothing like that.

He cocked his head to one side. "Please."

In the end, there was nothing rational about her decision. She didn't weigh how much she wanted the job against the unstable ground of attraction. She didn't calculate risk or benefit. She just heard the plea in his voice, saw how unhappy he looked, and thought of the peace she'd brought to him yesterday. She wanted to do it again. It was that simple.

Maybe that was wrong, wrong, wrong, but there had to be some higher power in the universe, some being that didn't believe in human suffering, that would forgive her.

"Get on the table."

"I like it when you're bossy."

She made a face at him. If he was going to flirt, that was going to make this ten thousand times harder. "Cut the BS."

"Sorry." He said it like he meant it. He slipped his hiking boots off and arranged himself on the table.

She started with the tapping, fingertips on his face.

"What *is* that? I mean, I get that it works, but I don't get how."

"Basically, I'm telling your body to tune in to the fact that you're holding tension. And also trying to distract your brain from the pain long enough for it to recognize that there *is* no pain."

"Oh, there's pain. You aren't trying to tell me that the pain's in my head, are you? Because I've heard that one too many times, thank you." One hand moved spasmodically on the table, but whether it was anger or whether she'd physically triggered the response, she couldn't tell.

"I'm trying to say that once the pain gets started, your brain is convinced it's there, even if whatever's causing the pain stops."

He nodded and closed his eyes. He had really long lashes for a guy. He'd shaved since yesterday, and that was somehow disconcerting, a step back toward the man who'd been so beautiful he'd seemed untouchable. Unattainable.

She'd never apologized in person to him for what had happened. Becca had told him the truth, and then Alia had sent him a brief but profuse apology email, thinking it was better to do it that way than to force him to confront her in the flesh. He hadn't written back, and she hadn't reached out to him again because she'd been sure he wanted nothing more to do with that episode of his life.

But something about how vulnerable and diminished he seemed—or maybe the fact that his eyes were closed—made it possible to bring up the past. "I haven't said—" she began, then stopped. "I'm sorry."

"No, you didn't hurt me," he said, his mind on the present moment, in which she was delivering stronger taps—karate chops, actually—to the tender spots where his arms met his torso.

"I mean, I'm sorry about deceiving you."

"Ohhhh."

She was pretty sure the "ohhhh" was for realizing what she was talking about, but it might also have been a groan of pleasure as she found an especially tight spot under his right shoulder blade. Her body, all amen about making him feel good, believed the latter.

"I still don't really understand why you did it," he said. "Wrote the letters. Or whatever. Cowrote the letters."

Because Becca needed *me to.*

"She has a learning disability. A cognitive disability. Like dyslexia, but... I don't know. They never really figured it out. She used to say that words 'wiggled' and 'crawled.' Even now that she's an adult, she needs help with anything written. She wanted you to like her, and she panicked about not being able to write you emails and letters the way she wanted to. So . . . so I helped her."

She'd left out the part of the explanation that went like this: *I've always taken care of Becca.*

Alia was the big sister, Becca the baby. Their father died when Alia was nine and Becca was six, and their mother went to bed and didn't get up. Alia shopped for food. She cooked dinner, did the laundry, braided Becca's hair, helped with homework. Eventually their mom rallied, but she never quite came back to them, and she frequently relapsed. Alia was never sure which mom she'd find, the weepy one who slept through daylight hours, or the functional one. So Alia got used to doing everything that had to be done: She made appointments with learning specialists, took Becca to those appointments on the city bus, listened as the experts admitted they were stumped by Becca's issues. Alia bought

Becca's Christmas presents (and her own). She crawled into Becca's bed at night, kissed her goodnight, heard her teenaged confessions, taught her how to use tampons, social media, condoms (though at 24, Becca still hadn't had occasion to use one). She picked her up after parties sodden drunk, dried her out, cleaned her up, set her back on her feet.

She didn't begrudge it. She felt, sometimes, resentful of their mother, but never of Becca. Becca needed her—

And Alia was there.

So writing Becca's letters had not seemed like a big deal. Not at first.

Nate opened his eyes, dark blue and, even upside down, curiously intense. That gaze provoked a queasy sensation in her stomach, a mix of lust and guilt.

"Why don't you roll onto your stomach. Here, give me a second, I'll get the face cradle."

She slid the face cradle into the end of the table and draped it with a towel. He rolled over with a sigh. She was reminded of a dog settling itself before a fire at night.

His glute muscles were gorgeously thick and tight. He was fully clothed in jeans and a T-shirt, but even so, there was way too much for her to admire. And when she began to stroke the long muscles in his back, her own body resonated.

She closed her eyes tight and did a reverse "Think of England." *I want this job. More than I want to slide my body up the length of his and comfort him with my warmth.*

I want this job more than that.

I do.

She could take refuge in her own shame over the past, too. "It was a big lie, what Becca and I did. In the beginning, I did my best to just write down what she said, but she kept asking, 'How could I say that better?' Or, 'Do you think that's what he meant?' Or, 'What would help him most?'"

And then, when Nate's replies came—*I know exactly what you mean; How did you know?; I feel like you know me so well*—Becca had said, *You see? What would I do without you? You know what to say to him.* She'd hugged Alia with gratitude.

Alia had tried to ignore her own joy at how he'd responded to *her* in the letter.

But somehow more and more of Alia had slipped into the letters. Thoughts she had about stories he'd told. Advice she wanted to offer him. Comfort in words Becca wouldn't have chosen but Alia eagerly typed up.

Toward the end, he'd written Becca a letter where he listed the things he missed most about civilian life. About Seattle. *The misty kind of rain where it's definitely raining but you can walk around in it without getting wet. Perfect summer days where you can sit in the sun without overheating. The Bon—sorry, Macy's!—star at Christmastime, and the carousel, too. Cow Chip cookies. Garlic fries and Kettle Korn at Safeco Field. And more generally, being at sports games. I was never a watch-it-on-TV guy. Always loved actually being there. I'd take an ordinary base-ball game with a couple friends over the World Series on a TV in a crowded room any day.*

"You should send him a care package," Alia told Becca.

"None of that stuff seems like it would travel very well."

"That's not the point," Alia said sternly. "The point is to cheer him up."

"It would be a lot of work."

It didn't seem that bad to Alia. And it would be fun, right?

Fun to think of his delight on opening the package. "What if I do the legwork? I don't mind."

"Sure, I guess. No harm, right?"

Alia took a photograph of the Macy's star and then, for good measure, she recorded some video of the carousel and the beaming (and terrified) children on it. She stored it all on a thumb drive shaped like the space needle.

She bought a RainGlobe. It was an-original-to-Seattle item that some enterprising lifelong resident had dreamt up.

There wasn't any way to capture a sunny day for him, but she did her best, photographing the sky in as many spots and from as many angles as she could, stitching them together in a collage.

She bought cookies and Kettle Korn. An old-school M's cap. *Had to leave out the garlic fries,* Alia wrote, on the printed note she included in the care package.

Several weeks later—during which she'd wondered, often, if he'd gotten the package and what expression he'd worn as he'd uncovered each treasure—she'd come home to the apartment to find Becca standing in the foyer, looking stricken. She held a sheet of paper in her hand.

"What?"

Wordlessly, Becca handed it to her. It was a long letter, full of stories about "the guys" and the long, painful wait that was Nate's war. *They're not kidding when they say it's ninety percent waiting, or whatever they say.*

But Alia knew it wasn't any of that that had made Becca's face look the way it looked. It was:

I'll be home somewhere around the end of April, and I want to see you so bad.

That care package might have been the nicest thing anyone's ever done for me. It's so lonely here, and it meant a ton to me to feel like someone out there gets me. You know? Sappiness alert: I was already falling for you, but that really sealed it.

It was the third week of April now. He'd be home, if everything had gone smoothly, in a week.

Falling for you.

Falling for—

Alia was struggling to assimilate all that she had learned in the last few minutes, and also struggling to figure out what it meant. Nate had said he was falling for *her,* meaning—

Suddenly, with a stab of pain, she saw. Saw it all, with total clarity.

Falling for someone, yes, but not Becca. And not her. Someone else. Someone who . . . didn't exist.

Lead sank in her gut. "Oh, shit."

"I thought it couldn't do any harm," Becca said slowly. "But I was wrong, wasn't I? Everyone said to wait till he came home. Everyone said you can't break up with someone who's deployed, it's too risky; if he's really upset, it could mess with his head, and then—"

The words coming out of Becca's mouth took a moment to make sense to Alia. They weren't the words she'd expected, the words about how the sisters had invented a woman and deceived a man, had deceived *Nate,* words about how angry he was going to be when he found out. They were different words.

"Wait. I don't understand. You want to break up with him?"

"I have to tell him the truth," Becca said. "I have to tell

him that it's not working for me, it's not going to work for me—"

How can Nate Riordan not work for you? He works overtime for me.

And as she—finally—heard the words echoing inside her head, she realized: It was true.

Even though she tried like hell not to think about him, tried to confine him to those moments when she was helping Becca. Even though she'd denied her feelings and buried herself in the composition of Becca's letters, the composition of *Becca,* as if a girlfriend was something you could craft. All the while lying to herself about the depth of her feelings, until she'd seen those words from him.

Falling for you.

She was in love with her sister's boyfriend.

Oh, Nate. *I've gone so far beyond falling. And—I've done a terrible thing.*

"I'll tell him everything," Becca was saying. "I'll tell him you helped with the letters. I'll show him the parts you helped with, and he'll see that he isn't really in love with me, and then maybe it will hurt less when I break up with him—"

Alia made a faint distressed noise, but she was pretty sure Becca was too far inside her own thoughts to hear her.

"I'm going to tell him you sent the care package, that *you* get him. Because you do. You always have. That's why you're so good with the letters."

And then Becca stopped. Held still, in a way that was deeper than Alia had ever seen anyone hold still. As if all the motion in all of the cells and vessels of her body had stopped, as if the whole world had stopped, as if she were listening to something far inside herself, and then her gaze sharpened on

Alia's face and the two of them were just standing there, staring into each other's faces, and it was like looking in a fun-house mirror, distorted reflections stretching infinitely in both directions, Becca's remorse—and Alia's no-longer-buried-longing.

"Alia—"

"Don't."

"You're in love with him."

"No. No."

"Did you—did you know you were?"

"No. I swear. I *swear*. Until—"

"God, I should have seen it! I can't believe I didn't see it! I'm an *idiot*. I understand why you couldn't see it. You probably didn't *want* to see it. But I should have! I would have—"

"You would have what?" Alia asked quietly.

They both stared at it, the futility of it.

He'd never been Alia's to give in the first place, and he wasn't Becca's to give "back." You couldn't just distribute a man like a gift. It had been a gross act of hubris, committed in the name of generosity.

"I'll tell him. I'll tell him the whole truth. Everything. I'll tell him how I feel, and how you—"

"No. No, please don't."

"Alia, why not? Maybe if he knows, then—"

But Alia was shaking her head, and her chest ached, because she understood. That there were some things about the human heart that made no sense. That you sometimes did wrong when you were trying to do good.

That it was too late.

"We can't just swap me in for you." Alia's voice sounded surprisingly calm to her own ears. "It doesn't work that way.

We invented a person, and we made him fall in love with her. And when we tell him the truth, we're going to take that away from him. He—" She caught her breath. "He won't forgive that."

"So—what do we do?" Becca whispered.

"We figure out the nicest, kindest, most truthful way for you to break up with him. And then—then we never do anything like that again."

A promise that, in the end, she hadn't kept.

On the physical-therapy table, Nate stirred and stretched almost luxuriously under Alia's hands, as if rising to meet her touch. She was jerked back to the present, her face reddening with remembered shame.

"I'm sorry," she said. It was pitiful and it was inadequate, but it was so, so true, and that somehow seemed like a good place to start. "I blame myself completely. I shouldn't have helped her. I should have pushed her away and told her she needed to do it herself. I was enabling when I should have made her face her issues."

I should have faced mine, too. A hell of a lot sooner.

"Well," he said dryly. "I'm glad you can see that now." And then, his voice muffled by the face cradle, "Hey. Don't beat yourself up over it. I get why you did it. And I'm over it."

Oh, God, if that wasn't the absolute *worst.* Because as much as she'd wanted his forgiveness—as much as she needed it—some part of her had secretly hoped he still mourned the lost connection. That he lay awake, maybe only on his worst nights, thinking of the woman who didn't exist, the perfect woman, the woman who'd written the letters and assembled the care package.

The woman who'd sent the instant messages.

Because as misguided and unlikely as it was, there was still a part of her that hoped that maybe, just maybe, he'd wake up from his trance and realize she was right here, in this room with him, flawed, misguided, and unglamorous, but real.

6

A few drops of drool had already dripped from his mouth, through the donut hole in the face cradle, and onto the floor of Alia's office. That was about as undignified as it was possible to get. Also distinctly unsoldierly.

But he'd never *been* a soldierly soldier. Not *really*. He'd done perfectly well acting the part of an alpha guy, but there had also been his love of writing, the journals he'd hidden, and his general sense that he *thought* more about things than most of the men he knew.

Which was why he'd loved those letters so much. They'd gotten that aspect of him, the artsy, thinky part that he mostly either denied or hid. She hadn't shied away from his doubts about whether he should have enlisted in the first place—whether it had been a mistake to think he could use the Army to pay off his debts without incurring brand-new, more emotionally weighty ones—or his feelings that just keeping his buddies alive didn't fill the giant chasm of *why*.

She.

Not Becca. Alia?

If it hadn't been immobilized in the face cradle, he would have given his head a shake to clear it.

He'd flat-out lied to her a minute ago, when he'd said it hadn't been a big deal. It had been a very big deal, discovering that the woman you'd thought you were in love with was a work of fiction. He'd thought he'd found the woman of his dreams—beauty and sex appeal, brains and a soul—and it had turned out she didn't exist. You didn't recover from that easily, and Alia was part and parcel of that pain, even if she hadn't been the only one to inflict the wound.

And even if she was making up for it now. She had amazing hands. Large and warm and strong and skilled. They moved with total confidence and accuracy, like she was reading him, reading the pain, and the pleasure, too. Following the thread of his relief, extending it and sweetening it. Right now she was working his lower back, and as it relaxed, he wanted her to knead lower, where the muscles in his ass were knotted.

Begging her to rub his butt would be even more undignified than drooling.

"I think it's really great. What you're doing, with the kayaking trip."

He shrugged, and something in his back and shoulder spasmed. He cursed.

"Easy. We don't have to talk about it if it's too hard." And without asking him where it hurt, she moved her hands from his lower back up to behind his shoulder blade and began to tap. And slowly, incrementally, the pain crawled back to where it had come from. Maybe only temporarily, but, Jesus, the relief of having someone who could track it down and chase it to its den—

It was easier than he would have thought to begin telling her the story.

"I couldn't keep sitting home, feeling sorry for myself, popping pills. And meanwhile, there's all this pomp and circumstance around my coming home, you know the stuff, 'Welcoming our heroes home!' and all that. And I kept thinking, it's so fu— so senseless. I mean, I lived and he died, and neither of those things was for a reason, and I wasn't a hero, just the one of the two of us that didn't die."

"Survivor guilt." Her hands had stopped momentarily, and she'd rested them, of all places, in his hair, her fingers moving slightly, restlessly, there.

"Yeah, yeah. That's what everyone says."

It was the feel of her fingers in his hair, maybe. Or how still she was, like she was waiting. Something made it possible to tell her the rest.

"I'd gotten to feel safe. We were on one of the more remote FOBs—forward operating bases—relatively little threat. Not like the other bases, where you'd hear about car bombings, insurgents shooting stuff out of tubes from the back of vehicles you couldn't even believe someone could still drive. And it wasn't like we were out on patrol. I'd done that, and that was fu — you never felt safe. But this—yeah, I knew we were in a war zone, but I didn't think— Anyway, stupid. You're never safe."

She inhaled sharply. But it was true. A fact of war.

"J.J. and I were doing guard duty. We were in the north tower, but nothing ever happened. We kidded around a lot. Told dirty jokes, talked about how much sex we'd have when we got home. They were eight-hour shifts, so it was inevitable that eventually one of us would head downstairs and outside to use the shi— latrine. In this case, he got up to go and I was like, *Dude, no, me first, I have to piss like a racehorse,* and he says, *Best of three,* so we shoot for it and I win. So that's what I was doing, dropping my helmet and my body armor at the base of the tower before I went into the latrine, because it was crazy hot and cramped in the Porta Potti. And then—"

Searing through his eardrums. His bones turned to metal and set to vibrate on a resonance that would shake him to bits. And the world rearranged.

As if she could read the pain as it ebbed and flowed, her hands moved over his scalp, his temples, the tender spots behind his ears, the place where his jaw was knotted tight.

"So you were downstairs when—" Softly.

"It was a rocket-propelled grenade. Yeah."

"And you feel like—"

"Like it should have been me. Maybe. Yeah. Sometimes. Even though I know I didn't do anything to make him die or to make myself live. It was just what happened. Just bad luck, you know? *Best of three.* But he had people he was responsible for. He was going to go home and help his dad run the hardware store, and eventually take over the business. He had Braden, and they'd planned this kayaking trip. It's like—"

He'd sat there one night, bottle of pills in his hand, and thought, *It was my turn to die. Not J.J.'s.*

"He was such a nice guy. The kind of guy everyone loved. And it was like I stole what was *his,* you know? I stole his luck. I felt *too* lucky. And I had to do something. There had to be some . . . some *point* to why I was the one alive. So I called Braden's grandparents—Braden's mom is out of the picture, wasn't ever in his life. They're great people. So strong. They're, like, so proud of J.J., and you know they're hurting, but they want everything good for Braden. I told them I wanted to do the trip with Braden and come work in the hardware store. I told them the situation, but promised I was getting clean. I swore to Braden's grandmother I'd get my act together and be a good role model, and she agreed to let me do the trip if I cleaned it up. She said to come see her in a couple weeks and we'd decide for sure. And so I quit the meds and then I came here. Because I figured if anyone could whup my ass into shape it was Jake."

"Only he's not here."

"You're doing an okay job."

She gave a short, surprised bark of a laugh. He liked making her laugh. She'd laughed a lot, the few times he'd hung out with her and Becca. Sometimes she'd seemed more alive and engaged than Becca had, but he'd told himself Becca was more the strong, silent type. Hidden depths. And the letters had borne that out. He'd *thought*.

"I didn't say this, but I was thinking—" He'd meant to stop talking, but words kept spilling out, like she'd loosened something in his head, too, not just all those muscles she was working. "Maybe I could do what J.J. had planned to do. Take over the hardware store eventually. Help provide for Braden if—I mean, his grandparents are young, like only late fifties, but I was thinking—"

J.J. had loved to brag about Braden. What a smart kid he was. How good at sports. On that one night when J.J. had been so talkative, he'd said, *All the clichés are true, you know. About kids. You just don't know. Until you have one. What love is.*

"But what about—"

For the first time since he'd seen her on the lake, she sounded a little uncertain.

"In the letters. You said—"

The letters. No wonder she was so halting. Because she wasn't supposed to have read the letters. She wasn't supposed to know everything she did about him.

For the first time, he didn't hate the thought of her having read them. Didn't hate the thought of her knowing things she wasn't supposed to know.

"You said when you were out of the Army, you wanted to work with troubled teenagers. Because you almost weren't going to go to college at all, because of the money, and then that teacher—what was his name?"

"James Harvey." He was a science teacher and basketball coach, and he'd refused to let Nate give up on a college education. Nate had thought of the guy every day in college. Every time he'd aced a test, passed a class, loved some piece of weird-ass philosophy he'd never have stumbled over if he'd decided to stop at a high school diploma. Every time he applied for a scholarship, a loan. When he'd signed on the dotted line with the Army, turned over the debt that otherwise would have crushed him, when he collected the checks that drew the debt down to a manageable level. He'd vowed he'd pay it forward somehow, someday.

"You could still do that. Start something for teens."

"If I worked for Braden's granddad and kept the store going, I'd be helping Braden."

She got quiet then.

Her hands resumed work, this time at his feet. She was finding spots on his feet and ankles that were reservoirs of stored anguish, then using what felt like a single knuckle to prod the pain out. The way you'd use a stick to grind a spark into ash. He'd never liked having his feet touched before. It always tickled. But what she was doing didn't tickle. It woke up the nerve endings, all right, but a different set.

"How's the pain?"

It had been flaring and subsiding as they talked and she worked, and there was relief in that, the way it could rise up and she could vanquish it again, a process that he could trust in. And then there was the way she listened, part and parcel with the gentleness of her hands and the sensitivity with which she ferreted out the places that held his suffering.

The way she touched him made connections between the corners and edges of him. Like she was mapping his whole body out, the outermost reaches, unexplored territories, and making them known.

He realized, with surprise and some alarm, that he was hard as a rock. His cock was partially tangled in his briefs, at a less-than-optimal angle, and flush, mad, *rioting* with blood. Okay, that was ridiculously inconvenient, and borderline embarrassing.

On the other hand, it wasn't totally shocking, right? There was a young, attractive woman with her hands all over him—in fact, now working her way up his legs in disturbing proximity to the unwanted action in his jeans.

Having the pain stop had been like that old saying about how good it feels to stop banging your head against the wall. Having someone touch him tenderly, listen to him patiently —those were bonuses.

Did his reaction mean he was hot for Alia?

Had he been, before?

He'd met her at Jake and Mira's picnic, found himself

spilling his guts in their first two minutes of acquaintance. Then she'd fled the scene, leaving him to chat with Becca.

But when he thought back on the picnic, when he really let himself think—

It was like twisting the knob on a microscope, memory coming back into focus. The way Alia had listened, not just with ears but eyes, too, her gaze under those long lashes. The contained energy of her, like she was holding something back. And he remembered, suddenly, wondering just what she was holding back, and how he could get her to unleash it.

The truth was, he'd been totally sucked into that conversation with her, had felt a speck of irritation, even, when Becca had interrupted them.

If she hadn't pushed her sister on him, what would have happened? Given five more minutes in her company, time to admire her smile, her eyes, her intelligence, her *spark,* five more minutes to wonder what lay buried beneath—what would have happened?

And there was the baseball game—

She and Becca had a third ticket to a Mariners game and had invited him to drive up from the base to attend with them. Becca had sat between them, and he'd spent a lot of time trying to restrain himself from PDAs, mostly involving the tantalizing gap between her dress and lace-clad breast. But when his mind hadn't been on groping Becca, he'd chatted with Alia. She was scoring the baseball game, which was a thing he'd always wanted to do but never known how to, and she explained the process, all eager and bright with excitement over the intricacies. She bought them beer and hot dogs: two each, drowned in mustard, ketchup, and relish, which—she explained happily—was how they were meant to be eaten.

Becca had been quiet that day, had let Alia jabber joyfully and discourse on baseball and the proper doctoring of hot dogs. He hadn't, he realized, interacted with Becca much until he'd gotten her alone later, and then they hadn't done much talking. And yet he'd had a blast that day. It had become a bright spot in his memory, one of those days his heart reached for when he thought about times he'd been happy. He'd always attributed his joy that day to baseball and Becca.

But now he wondered.

What if there had been more time? More conversations. More baseball games, more of that giddy joy on Alia's face. What if he'd gotten a chance to witness her kindness and learn the workings of her mind? To admire the smattering of freckles across her nose, and the strength in her lean but curvy body?

What if he'd known the letters were from her?

On the other hand, maybe he was just suffering from long-term sexual deprivation—it had been nine months solid since he'd gotten laid, and what red-blooded American male wouldn't appreciate some massage by that point?

It was probably just stupid penis stuff. Pretty much any woman could get to him right now.

Right?

7

"Hey, baby sister." Alia tucked the phone audio bud into her ear so she could jog the woods path while she talked to Becca. It was a typical morning near the Oregon coast, fog lying cool and low over the treetops. A mist, like the Seattle one Nate had written about, wrapped itself against her skin like an embrace.

"Hey, big sister," Becca returned.

They always greeted each other that way. They'd been doing it forever. Alia couldn't even remember anymore when it had started.

"Don't mind the heavy breathing. I'm talking to you while I run."

"I won't take it personally." Becca paused. "I heard a vicious rumor. Just calling to confirm it's not true."

"Oh, yeah?" Alia kept her voice light.

"I heard Nate Riordan is there."

They hadn't talked about Nate, not once, since the breakup. Becca had mentioned his name, raised the topic, made it clear she was open to hearing the whole story—but Alia had always found a way to change the subject.

"Mira emailed me from Hawaii. She wanted me to check on you and make sure you were okay."

Mira knew only the vague outlines of the story. That Alia had helped with the letters, that things had ended awkwardly. But it was so Mira to be worried about Alia's well-being. She was everyone's mom.

"Is he your *patient*?"

"I can neither confirm nor deny."

Becca laughed. "Well, if he is, that must be awkward."

If Alia had been able to talk about it to Becca—if it hadn't been a) sealed in the virtual patient vault, and b) buried under layers of Alia's own guilt—she would have said:

Not awkward, exactly. Surprisingly not awkward.

More—compelling.

Addictive.

Even in motion, her feet pounding the pine needle–covered path, her body heated up, thinking about how it felt. To stand over him, to have his body be hers to soothe. To give pleasure to.

You're not sublimating.

Go to hell.

"I still feel so bad about what I did to him." Becca's voice was soft.

"What *I* did to him."

"Okay, fine—what *we* did. We were both responsible. God, I want to call him up sometimes and apologize like it's going out of style."

Nate had made it sound yesterday like he was over it, but

that was privileged info, too, having been conveyed on the table.

"I still wish—" Becca hesitated. "I just wished I'd paid more attention. At the picnic. I wish I'd known you were into him—"

"Oh, sweetie," Alia said. "Stop. Please. It's ancient history. I'm *fine*." The last thing she wanted was for Becca to still be beating herself up over it.

"I wish I hadn't *asked* you to write the letters. I wish I'd bucked up and had a little more confidence in myself. Because we hurt him. And because—because you were in love with him and we ruined any chan—"

"Hush," Alia said. "It's fine. And honestly, I think he was more angry than hurt." She responded to that part of what her sister had said so she didn't have to address the other part.

"Is he still?"

"Not sure." He'd sent her such mixed signals. His anger at the lake and then his dismissal of the topic as no big deal.

"I wish you'd told him that you had feelings for him," Becca said quietly. "After everything came down."

Alia wanted her sister to let it go already. The pity in Becca's voice made her cringe. "It wouldn't have made any difference."

"Wouldn't it?"

"I don't think so." Actually, she knew it wouldn't have, because he *had* known about the care package and the IMs, enough to piece together the truth if it had been a welcome one. "He wanted someone who didn't exist."

"I don't think we gave him a chance to know what he wanted."

Alia's heart skipped a beat, but she made herself be sensible. Nate had had plenty of time to think about what he wanted, and he'd given no sign of regret.

I'm over it, he'd said.

"Besides, it doesn't matter. Even if it weren't for that, he's —" She cut herself off.

"Your patient."

"I can neither con—"

"Got it," Becca said with a laugh. There was a long silence. Then she said, "Say hi from me. And tell him I'm sorry. Or don't, actually. That would be incredibly awkward and ironic, huh? If you apologized for me?"

"Hell, yeah."

Alia stretched out her stride, her muscles warm now, the path underfoot soft with needles.

"So . . . I have a little bit of crazy news myself." Becca's dreamy sigh brushed Alia's eardrum. "I met someone."

"Someone—" Alia didn't dare let herself hope Becca meant what it sounded like she meant. The One.

"We've been out twice. I think Friday's the big night."

"Are you sure? Just because it's the third date doesn't mean—" Alia knew Becca felt like the oldest virgin on earth, and she was eager to get rid of that particular albatross. Alia worried that she was a little too eager.

"Alia!"

"Sorry!" The mothering habit died hard. And Becca— well, Becca had a knack for getting in her own way. Alia had heard this early excitement from her before, but somehow, things didn't quite jell. "Just . . . make sure you're ready."

"Sister, dearest, you need to worry more about getting yourself laid and less about me."

Touché. She sped up her pace a little.

"I don't think I'll be getting laid anytime soon."

"Yeah, no nooky with *any* of the patients, huh?"

"Nope."

"That's a lot of off-limits soldier flesh."

A vivid picture of Nate, facedown on her table, flashed through her head before she could banish it. "Indeed. And quit stalling. Are you going to tell me about your first and second dates or what?"

Becca's sweet laugh cut through everything else and brought Alia back to herself, as it so often did.

"HEARD A STORY THE OTHER DAY." Nate regarded his shitty poker hand darkly, then folded. Griff and Chaucer were locked into some kind of pissing contest, big bets and lots of posturing. Tron sat back in his chair, looking amused. Probably it would turn out he had something worthwhile, and the other two guys were in it for the buzz.

"Turk, you know him? Last deployment, he had this deal with a buddy. The buddy had a family, and Turk didn't, so Turk would always take dangerous jobs, missions, trips, whatever, so the friend could get home safe. Turk kept dodging bullets, and then one day, Turk was, like, two minutes too late to board a Hawk for a recon mission and so his friend went instead—"

"You don't fucking *make* those kinds of promises." Tron was bolt upright now, and angry.

"Chopper crashed?" That was Griff.

"Of course it fucking crashed," Tron said. "It crashed, right?"

Nate nodded.

"You make a promise you couldn't keep?" Nate asked Tron quietly.

"Way too fucking many of them, man."

All the men went silent. Probably thinking about promises, the ones they'd made in words—*Baby, I'll come home to you, safe and whole. I've got your back, man. Leave this up to me*—and the unspoken ones, too. The promise you made when you said goodbye to family, that you'd try not to get yourself killed. The promise you made to the guy at your side by virtue of standing next to him. The promise you made to yourself that you'd get J.J. home to his family, somehow or other, and that if you couldn't do that, you'd find some other way to take care of the people he'd left behind.

Talking to the men here—it was dark. Dark, darker, darkest. Since he'd arrived, Nate had heard more heartbreaking stories than he had in all the rest of his active time put together. They were currency here—what you'd seen and done, what had happened to your friends over there and back home. And there were stories even when the men were shut down and silent, even the men who wouldn't talk about war or who wouldn't talk at all. You *felt* the stories.

He tried to imagine telling these guys what he was thinking, about promises and about *feeling* stories, but he figured they'd either stare at him like he'd grown two heads or laugh. Not in a mean way, just in a *WTF, dude?* way. They might even think he was kidding.

Alia, though. He could tell her. She'd get it.

Huh.

Griff won the hand and raked the chips into the growing heap in front of him. "I had a friend who came home and his wife didn't meet him at the field and then when he got a ride home he discovered that the house was empty. Like empty empty. She'd moved herself and all her furniture out, and it was just him, sitting in this goddamn empty house. His buddies took turns doing suicide watch for weeks on him. He's okay, though. I mean, you know, okay as it goes."

"Jesus," said Nate. "That *sucks.*"

"It hacks me off." Griff sounded pissed now. Didn't take much to light the fuse of most of the vets Nate knew. "It's the same women who think they want a soldier. The ones who go soldier hunting in bars and get pregnant on purpose. They're the worst. Then you come home and you're not what they wanted at all. You're all broke-ass and fucked up, and they're like, 'I just wanted a cute guy in a uniform,' and you're like, 'Then why didn't you bang a firefighter, sweetheart?'"

His voice had grown tight, the words percussive.

They all looked at him.

Tron crossed his arms and stared Griff down. "That was you. You were the one with the empty house."

Griff looked away, but you could read it in the lines of his face. The whole goddamn story. If they'd been somewhere else, Nate would have bought the guy enough drinks to make him forget, maybe tried to get him laid, but they were here, and they had cards and stories and the comfort of knowing they'd all done the same stupid shit—made promises and believed promises made to them. So he said what they were all thinking: "That sucks."

Griff nodded. And Tron said, "You think the Seahawks are going to the Super Bowl again this year?"

Because. Because you moved on, or you got stuck stewing in it.

But Nate kept thinking about it, about Griff's wife, and how she'd broken her promise. How she hadn't been who he'd believed she was. And about Becca, and those crazy hybrid letters, which had made him lose his mind with longing. He'd come home on leave, feeling like he *had* to see her. Had to show her how much he'd come to care. Had to tell her he'd fallen in love with her.

Her—Becca, that is.

He'd ignored the dissonance that had been there from the very beginning. His vague discomfort, the unsettling sense that the letters didn't *match*. He'd gone back to Afghanistan feeling *fond. Affectionate.* He'd had a good time with Becca, he'd found her good company, if not terribly lively. Drawing her out, getting her to tell him, for example, what she'd thought of a movie they'd seen together—it had been *work*. And not the most rewarding work, either. She was timid, unwilling to express too strong an opinion. She'd seemed a little afraid of him. Afraid of herself.

Unlike the letter writer. So much gutsiness and strength in those letters, no fear of broaching any topic at all. No fear of him. Opinions aplenty. *There's no shame in bailing when your time's up. You should be doing something you love.*

He'd somehow missed the echo of his conversation with Alia at the picnic. How could he have missed that?

Does it help at all to know I think you're a really good person, even if some days you wonder?

Not words that would have come out of Becca's mouth, or off the end of her pen. How could he have missed *that*?

The letter writer wasn't someone you could feel fond of.

Not someone you could feel lukewarm toward. She was someone you could *crave*. She was someone who could make waiting a few days for a flight out feel like an eternity.

And then there was the kissing.

Kissing Becca had been—lukewarm, he'd have to say. Uninspired. Becca had been meek and self-conscious in his arms, willing but passive, but the woman on the other end of those letters had known exactly what she wanted.

He'd told her. Becca. It was one of the first things he'd said to her when he got off the plane, after another of those surprisingly uninspired kisses, a huge disappointment after all the built-up anticipation.

I feel like you're really different from your letters. I feel like we're *really different from how we were in those letters.*

She'd gotten this look on her face. And he'd started to backpedal, not wanting her to feel like it was a criticism, when all he was trying to say was, *I wish you'd let her come out, that woman you are on paper. I wish you'd be more that way in person. I know you have it in you. Maybe if we work together, we can close the gap.*

Then, slowly, haltingly, awkwardly, so apologetically, she'd told him the truth.

It had taken the breath out of his chest. He understood the cliché *crushed* for the first time.

But *he should have known.*

"Nater?"

He wasn't sure where that nickname had come from. He'd always been straight-up Nate with his squadmates, even though a lot of the other guys had nicknames.

"Just thinking."

"One more hand?"

"Sure, what the fuck."

He suddenly remembered something he'd made himself forget. Made himself block out, because it had been so much part and parcel of his disappointment.

That last instant message exchange, with *MenInUni242*. God! How could he have forgotten those?

I want your tongue all over me.

I want you to pin me down.

I want your cock in my mouth. As much as I can hold.

He'd been shocked by her boldness. Because of the contrast with how she—*Becca*—had been in his arms.

And so when Becca had told him the truth, that had been one of the first things he'd thought of—*Ohhh. Right.*

Not Becca's words. Made-up words. Fictional words.

But now he saw it differently.

Alia's words.

Holy shit.

This probably wasn't going to help him much with the wood-on-the-PT-table problem.

8

At lunchtime most days, Alia swam across the lake and back. It took her about half an hour at an easy pace, so she estimated it was probably a quarter-mile in each direction. It was part exercise and part meditation, the sameness of the strokes, her fingers cutting through water, the quiet under the surface, only the bubbling of her exhalations audible. She could *think* under there, or, rather, *not think,* which was the point. To empty her brain, which lately had been jumping around like a monkey on her.

Maybe I should tell Nate the truth.

The truth being the fact that she had, once upon a time, loved him. That the letters had held so much of her, that the care package and the IMs had been all her, and only her. No fictional amalgam.

He'd told her so much the other day, the way it had felt to hit bottom, why the kayaking mattered to him, the exact shape of his survivor's guilt. *I didn't do anything to make him die or to make myself live. It was just what happened.* And then—

offhand, as if it weren't the thing he thought about most: *He was such a nice guy, the kind of guy everyone loved.*

She knew what he was really saying was, *If it had to be one of us, it should have been me.*

Of course, there was nothing fair, not from a human perspective, about who lived and who died—not on or off the battlefield. But that wasn't what he needed to hear.

She'd almost said it. *You're that kind of guy, Nate. The kind of guy everyone loves. And I know, because I—*

"Wait *up.*" A shout loud enough to cut through the water in her ears.

Murphy's Law of Empty Lakes, she thought. *The guy you're thinking about is the one gaining a length per second on you.*

He reached her and they treaded water. "You look great," she said.

Jake was due back in three days. Nate had grown stronger; the dark shadows had faded from under his eyes, and his skin had bronzed—but that wasn't what she meant. She meant that he moved more easily, as if pain were no longer his constant companion.

She'd given him a regimen of stretching and strengthening, cardio to keep inflammation low and endorphins high, and loads of water to drink. But she'd also done everything she could to keep him off her table and out of her quiet office. If pain surfaced when he was working with her in the open, central physical therapy area, she gave him more stretches, encouraged him to tap with a tennis ball on the tense spot, or sent him to the hot tub (without her). She told herself she was building his confidence, his independence, but the truth was, she was scared of him. Or, really, she was scared of herself. Of how badly she wanted to cross the line, slide a hand under his T-shirt, under the waistband of his jeans, between his thigh and the table, over his flat abs, up, down —everywhere.

And this—alone in the middle of a lake, mostly naked— was not an improvement.

"Looks like you're going to be fine to do the trip, huh?" she asked. They were bobbing up and down the way one did when treading water and conversing. She wondered what her breasts were doing under her sporty swimmer's suit, and whether they were too small altogether to register with him.

He shook his head. "I have to get to the point where the pain is more under control. It keeps jumping out at me."

"That's going to happen for a while. The trick is not to get into a fear-pain cycle when that happens—not to let yourself tense up and make the pain worse. Can you just . . . I know this sounds funny, but *accept* the pain?"

He gave her a scornful look. "You try accepting it. It *hurts.*"

"I know. But it *is* something you can learn to do. That's the basis of a lot of pain-reduction techniques. I'm leading this morning meditation cir—"

"I don't meditate."

"You also didn't want to do PT," she pointed out.

"I don't meditate."

It had been a tough sell to the other men, too, at first. She'd meditated alone the first four mornings after she'd stared her "circle." But she'd stuck it out, and they'd begun to show up.

"The Seattle Seahawks do it. And I just read an article about Marines who've started doing it. To help with battle strain."

He gave her a look, as if to say, *What the fuck does that have to do with me?*

"Three guys came this morning, including Griff."

His eyebrows went up.

"Yep, Griff," she said smugly. "I think you should try it. It'll help you feel like you have a better relationship with the pain."

"See? It's when you say stuff like that that I can't take you seriously at all. *A better relationship with the pain?*"

"Just try it."

He shook his head. "No, thanks. I'll do it my way, thank you very much."

She shrugged and got a mouthful of water for her trouble. "Are you going all the way across?"

"Was thinking of trying."

He fell in beside her. They swam side by side, and that was good, too. There was the quiet, and the steady, peaceful rhythm, and then there was his company, which should have unsettled her but felt like a tether. She'd never liked the deep, dark middle of the lake much, but with him next to her, it bothered her less.

They were closing in on the far shore when she realized she'd lost him and turned to see him struggling.

She swam swiftly back, and he grabbed for her, but she moved out of his way, afraid he'd pull her under in his panic and drown both of them. From her high school lifeguarding days, she remembered: There was nothing more dangerous than a panicked swimmer. "You're okay," she said, soothingly. "You're okay."

"It hurts." He was flailing like he'd never swum a stroke in his life.

"You're okay. Turn on your back."

He was beyond hearing her, still reaching desperately for her.

"Nate!" She wasn't sure where the drill-sergeant voice had come from. "Turn. On. Your. Back."

Damn it, she'd slap him if she had to.

He flopped himself onto his back and, bit by bit, stilled his struggles.

For a moment, the only sound was his breathing, fast and rough, then slowing gradually as he registered that he was going to be okay.

She had to take a minute to calm her own breathing, too. Only then did she let herself realize how far away from shore they still were. How big the sky was over their heads, their two little selves in this blue vastness. Note to self: Maybe it wasn't the smartest thing on earth to swim all alone out here.

"What happened?" she asked.

He'd been caught off guard by his pain, the way he'd described earlier. "I panicked, and I kept going under." There was a kind of wonder in his voice. "That's never happened to me. I'm a strong swimmer."

"I think it can happen to anyone if they panic."

They swam slowly to shore and climbed out of the water. She led him into the sunny clearing, where she liked to sit on a big log and dry out.

"You see? I can't kayak by myself with a little kid. I'll scare the crap out of him. And what if I need to rescue *him,* and I panic like that again?"

"If you had to, you'd do it. You let me help you because I was there, but if the situation had been reversed, you would have snapped out of it."

He shook his head. "I don't know. *Fuck.*"

"It hurts?"

"Will you tap?"

They were alone in a clearing that was so quiet and peaceful and beautiful it was like a chapel. Tall trees, firs and cedars, towered overhead, but there was enough of a space here that sunlight filtered down and warmed the air, warmed the ground, warmed the log where they were sitting, and warmed their bodies. Or maybe it was his warmth she felt.

She knew she shouldn't do it, but she knew where his pain was and how to make it go away. So she did it.

She used her fingertips, loose and gentle, to tap a rhythm on the strong muscles of his neck and down the long, lean muscles that defined the groove of his spine. The bare, damp cap of one shoulder, starting to turn gold from regular sun exposure. The front of that shoulder, the length of his collarbone, and then, at some point, without meaning to, she simply gave herself over to it, to whatever he needed. She exhaled deeply, long, deliberate sighs to remind him to breathe. Clenched a handful of his shoulder where the tension had to be coaxed out. Brushed long strokes of her palms over the planes of his back—because. Because that was what he needed.

Because that was what *she* needed.

9

I t turned out that Alia was shockingly sexy in a bathing suit, all curves and long, strong limbs, and a pale powdering of freckles all over. Hair streaming, drops of water sparkling on her bare skin—and her demeanor, too: powerful and certain, but calm and peaceful.

He'd noticed that about her before. Sometimes it seemed like she was absorbing his pain directly, soaking the hurt into her vast tranquillity, like wide-open blue sky, where everything small got lost.

He'd told himself he wanted only her hands on his body. He loved her touch. He was greedy, like a kid who wants his mom to stay and keep rubbing his back at bedtime.

That was why he'd asked her to tap. That was why he was sitting here now, as she moved around him, tapping, stroking, squeezing, digging her strong knuckles and fingertips into the give of his muscle. Because he was greedy for human contact, for soothing touch.

He felt her breath brush across the back of his neck as she worked on his shoulder. He shivered.

She stopped and sat beside him on the log. "You cold?"

"I'm okay. You?"

"Freezing," she admitted.

She was covered with goosebumps. He took one of her hands. "Ice. We should swim back."

But neither of them moved.

He wanted to push the damp piece of hair off her forehead. And he wanted to play dot-to-dot with the freckles on her shoulder, following them to where they disappeared under the strap of her bathing suit.

Huh.

The way she looked now, shoulders exposed, speckled with the sun's gold glow, reminded him of the way she'd looked that day at the picnic. The way *he'd felt*. Words spilling out of him like they had on the table, like he couldn't hold himself back from her.

She'd rescued him earlier, maybe even saved his life, with no more rustling of her surface calm than she showed in the PT office. *This is what needs to be done. Here. Done.* No nonsense.

He was suddenly filled with such a deep gratitude that it felt uncontainable. Unmanageable.

He wanted to lick the drops of water off her throat. And off her breastbone above the swell of her breasts, which were way too well guarded by that high-necked suit. Except for her nipples, whose exact shape and degree of hardness were vividly revealed. He wanted to peel down the top of the suit so he could toy with them and find out what color they were and what sound she would make when he drew one into his mouth and flicked his tongue against it.

He wanted to take her in his arms and warm away the

goosebumps. He wanted to know if she'd whimper when he kissed her, if she'd yield or push back, if she'd protest about her job and if he could stop those protests with his mouth.

He wanted to know how the woman in front of him connected with the woman who'd written the letters and stocked the care package and—maybe—typed those instant messages.

He reached out his hand, hesitated for a fraction of a second, then pushed the strand of hair off her forehead.

She made a small, uncertain sound and drew back.

The world hung, suspended. And then, without deciding, he decided.

"You make me feel so good," he whispered. "I want to do that to you." He wove his fingers into her wet hair and drew her toward him.

And he kissed her. Her mouth was cool and still at first, and then warm, and then hot, and mobile, and greedy. Her hands came to his back, to the back of his neck, but not the way they'd always come before. She wasn't stroking or tapping or reprogramming his pain response. She was demanding. More, deeper. Giving him her tongue, taking his. And playful. Nipping, teasing, drawing back, then letting him have her again. So good. He tugged her onto his lap, desperate to feel the press of her almost-naked body against his. The cool length of her thigh against the way-too-hot—

She broke away. "Nate."

He took her wrists. "I *need* this. Can we do this now and regret it after?"

"Oh, *God,*" she said, and for a blissful split second she didn't resist, and he felt her breath brush his lips before she pushed back with both hands. "No, Nate, I can't. I *can't*." She got up and walked away, facing the lake, her back to him.

As if that, somehow, was supposed to cool his ardor. But honestly? There was no view of her that wasn't tempting. Her waist was slim, and her ass—*Aw, not fair.* "Because you're treating me?"

She hesitated, then nodded. She turned to face him, her cheeks pink. "PT code of conduct forbids sexual contact between PT and patient. And Oregon law backs it up with threats to my license, fines, all sorts of stuff."

She sounded like she was reading from a speech. All starch and bluster.

If it hadn't been for her *Oh, God* earlier, he might have let it go. He might have assumed that protesting about her job was her way of saying *no* gracefully. But that *Oh, God* had come straight from the soul. It had been breathless and needy and grateful—she'd liked what he'd said, about making her feel good. She liked that he wanted her. She wanted him, too. He wanted to plunge into the center of that *Oh, God.* He wanted to be there with her, at that flash point.

"But if *I* kiss *you*—"

Her eyes got big and dark at that, but she shook her head. "The law says it doesn't matter who initiates. I'll have to stop treating you."

That was like a giant bucket of cold water.

"Why?"

"Because it's wrong for me to treat you and . . . let you kiss me."

He wondered what she'd been about to say. Whether her mind, like his own, had leapt ahead to all the things he wanted to do next. Lick the trail of freckles across her shoulder. Take the strap of her bathing suit in his teeth. Lower the suit to reveal what was underneath. Drink his visual fill.

Parts of him were already screaming demands—*more, more, all!*—and he meant what he'd said, that he wanted her to feel it, too, the pleasure of being taken care of, the sense of having the weight of her own self lifted off her, the rush of released tension. The afterglow.

The other part of him was panicking at the thought of losing the relationship he already had with her. He needed the woman who stood over him on the table, drew the map for him, listened as he talked, even when what came out of his mouth was as ragged and unmapped as his hurting body.

Maybe there was a way, though, to have it all. "What if you let me kiss you, but you don't officially treat me? Like you just help me out from time to time, unofficially."

She made a face. "Even if you're my ex-patient, I'm not supposed to seek a relationship with you."

"So, what, if you meet someone and you're really attracted to them, you're supposed to ignore it?"

She nodded. "Pretty much. I mean, there's wiggle room in the law—"

He'd taken a step forward almost without meaning to. "If there's wiggle—"

She held a hand up to stop his advance. "No, but not in *this* situation. I mean, first of all, way too weird, right? Because of what happened—"

He waved it away. "Forget that."

An emotion flashed across her face, one he couldn't read, and she turned away for a moment. Then back, expression set, determined. "You're here for what, six weeks? Minus the weekend you're away with Braden. And then you're off to help J.J.'s parents. And I'm trying to convince Jake to give me a job here. I want to *stay* here. And there might be wiggle room in the law, but let's face it, I'm not going to get hired at a new job if my first act on being given a two-week trial period is to totally lose all control."

"All control, huh?" What a pretty picture that made. And again, the words of her sexts—officially, Becca's sexts—crossed his mind. How much of *MenInUni242* was in Alia Drake?

"Nate. I really want this job. This is what I'm supposed to be doing. I'm good at it. Guys like you—they *need* me."

He did need her. The idea that if he crossed this line, he might lose access to her completely—he hated that idea.

So he might very well not find out how much of *MenIn-Uni242* was in Alia. Not now. Maybe not ever.

He hated that idea, too.

THAT KISS HAD ALMOST SHORTED out her brain. The heat of his mouth, the sureness of his lips and tongue moving against hers.

She'd thought (before thought had vanished):

Holy, holy, holy, holy—

And, *Oh my God—*

He's kissing me. Me. The real *me.*

Because after all this time, even though she'd done her best to ruin things—this was happening. The sweep and tingle, the claiming, the grip of his hands on her shoulders, his breath rough wherever it touched her.

And then, as if that hadn't been enough, she'd felt the

biggest, hardest, most indisputable evidence that he needed her. It had almost made her want to cry with longing.

She had pushed him away, but her mind had jumped ahead even as she had, wanting to rock against him, to try to work herself closer to him. To straddle him. They were wearing so little clothing. His bathing trunks and that teeny-tiny strip of her own bathing suit, which his kiss alone had turned into a wet mess between her legs. She would straddle him and he would twist that strip of fabric aside and thrust into her, just like that, while she was sitting in his lap.

They could almost pretend they weren't doing what they were doing, then. They could almost pretend that she hadn't ever deceived and hurt him, that their being together now wasn't breaking rules and risking a friendship and a career.

He'd be big and he'd fill her and she'd rock on him and slide on him until all the tension and pain drained away. Until the past drifted out of view—

Yeah, so not sublimating.

He was nodding.

"Okay," he said.

Damn it, that was the answer she was supposed to *want.* That was the correct answer. That was the answer that would allow her to keep treating him—which was the best thing for him. It was the answer that would allow her to keep working toward a real job at R&R—which was the best thing for her.

So why did she feel so disappointed?

The look in his eyes when he'd said, *I need this.* She was trying to think if anyone had ever looked at her quite like that. Like she was the answer to a prayer. The missing piece of some cosmic puzzle. And she'd thought it was heady taking away his pain. She'd thought it was addictive to make him feel good. But this was something else entirely. That look in his eyes had hinted at the fact that she could make him feel *better* and *best, too,* and her body had wanted desperately to take a shot at giving him that.

Her body *still* wanted a shot at that.

Stupid bodies.

"We should—head back."

"You feel good enough?"

"Yeah," he said. "Funny. Pain's gone."

Not funny at all, she thought. *Oxytocin.* That was the sex hormone, the very same hormone that his drug of choice had been artificially crafted to resemble. Great natural painkiller. An orgasm would produce even more of it—

Okay, that was not a thought she should have allowed herself to have. Because it had conjured a way-too-vivid picture of how blissed-out she could make Nate, if she gave him what she knew he needed.

It was time to get away from here.

Stepping back into the lake, she was hyperconscious of her body. The cold water heightened the sensation of heat between her legs, made her internal muscles draw up against the icy touch. Her nipples, already painfully hard, tightened even more. And that sent another current of pleasure into her low belly. One kiss. He'd *kissed* her and she was raring to go.

And then, as they struck out across the lake, him setting the pace, she had to admit something else to herself. She wished he'd pushed back harder. She wished he'd overcome her resistance. She wished he needed her *so damn much* that he decided all the rest didn't matter.

Holy hell, she was in trouble.

And the thing was, none of this should surprise her. She

knew from the past how good she was at deceiving herself and how bad she was at resisting him. And she had just done both again.

God, she was an idiot.

She made up her mind. She would stay as far away from him for the next three days as humanly possible. And when Jake came back, she would tell him, *Let's transfer Nate's care to you. He kissed me, and I don't think I should treat him.* That would be enough truth for her to feel like she wasn't lying, without risking her future employment at R&R. She'd help get Jake up to speed on what was working best for Nate's care, but it would be Jake laying hands on Nate's smooth, golden skin from this point forward. Temptation removed.

What a relief that would be.

10

He packed up a duffel bag and drove himself the four hours down to Eagle Hill, where Jim, Suzy, and Braden lived.

The drive gave him too much time to think. He'd woken up knowing he had to get away. He hadn't slept. He hadn't been able to get her out of his head. Not the taste of her mouth or the way she'd half climbed into his lap or her *Oh, God* or the scent of her, rich and sweet in the air. He'd thought he'd been sleepless before, but last night had been something new altogether. He'd jerked off *twice* in the silent dark, just to have a few minutes respite from wanting her.

Horny and pissed—an awesome combination.

She'd responded to him. Without thinking, she'd reacted to the touch of his mouth. She'd kissed and licked and *wanted* more. She'd been ready to take more, before good sense had prevailed.

That had gotten him going so fast—

And then she'd been all *No way.* And he just didn't get it. Because he'd told her he'd forgiven her for the past. And she'd said herself there was wiggle in the rules. So if they liked each other, why couldn't it all be okay? Then he could haul her onto his lap again, but this time do everything he wanted to her.

Although he agreed with her on one count. This couldn't go anywhere. She loved this job and he was going to work for Jim and Suzy. They couldn't really hope to have anything between them other than a few rolls in the hay. The whole reason he'd put himself in Alia's hands was so he could be there for J.J.'s family. For Braden and Jim and Suzy, for the store, for J.J. Alia wasn't the end, she was just a means.

When he finally pulled up outside the little ranch house in Eagle Hill, once he'd hauled his duffel inside, J.J.'s mom all but made him pee in a cup, quizzing him about how long he'd been clean and how he was feeling. Then she let him take Braden out kayaking. They rented boats and stayed out most of one afternoon.

Braden was cool. He was ten, a little boy one minute and a man the next. The grief came and went, too, bursts of anger Nate could see were bigger than his frustration with not being able to turn as easily as he wanted, or getting his paddle wrapped up in lake weeds. Nate didn't try to talk to him about J.J. They'd have time on the longer trip, plenty of time for big conversations. Maybe Braden would ask Nate about J.J. then. In the last few years, Nate had spent more time with J.J. than Braden had, a fact he was acutely conscious of. It sucked that he'd gotten the best and last years of J.J.'s life.

When he wasn't out with Braden, he helped Jim in the store. They talked about how when Nate's time at R&R was up, he'd come to work there, but they didn't discuss what would happen long term. Nate didn't tell him that he was thinking he should be the one to fulfill J.J.'s mission, to keep the business alive until Braden was old enough to take over.

Between times, he did his PT exercises diligently, strengthening. Stretching. Things were different now, more space behind his shoulder blades, more separation between the individual knots that made up his spine. When he couldn't make a muscle let go, he tapped on it with a tennis ball he'd brought with him.

The pain came and went, but it seemed less—angry. Less *personal*. Less stubborn.

Over Suzy's obscenely good meatloaf and garlic mashed potatoes, she asked a million questions.

"So you grew up near Seattle?"

"Port Orchard. Across the Sound."

"Brothers, sisters?"

"I was an only. My mom's great—she was a single mom, but she worked like a dog to take care of me, but managed to still have time to be the fun mom."

"And your—"

"My dad was a firefighter. He died when I was four, in a fire."

Their eyes met, acknowledging what they shared. He could see the sadness that would probably never leave her, and he didn't kid himself that he could make it go away. He wasn't J.J., and he'd never be J.J. But maybe he could be something. Some help, some consolation. Like a rope bridge over a chasm.

"What'd you study in college?"

"Nonprofit management."

"Store's profitable, though," Jim said. He was a man of few

words and rare smiles. Nate wondered if he'd smiled more. Before.

"It's all the same. Business." Which wasn't true, of course, but he didn't want them thinking he was sacrificing something for them. Making them feel guilty was the opposite of the point.

"But you must have chosen that degree for a reason," Suzy said. "You must have had plans. Ideas."

"Well, sure, but plans change."

He *had* had plans, but, then, so had J.J. What was that thing people said? Life was what happened while you were busy making other plans.

Or death was what happened.

"And how about love? Is there someone—special—in your life now?"

He saw Alia in his mind's eye, clear as water, the way she'd looked that first day in the kayak, fierce and beautiful. She had somehow found her way into all his senses. When he thought about her, he thought about the way she'd felt in his arms beside the lake, the way she'd tasted and smelled. Even when he couldn't see her or touch her, he could still hear her, the sound of her voice as her fingertips probed his sore muscles, and the sound of her silence when she was listening.

Suzy regarded him, that sadness there again, and the sensual surround experience of Alia shattered. Because he knew what Suzy was thinking. That there would never be someone special for J.J.

"No," he said. "No one special."

And then they'd talked about J.J. About how he could always make them laugh. About how he wasn't afraid of anything. Suzy said he never had been, that he'd scared the shit out of her as a kid, climbing fifty feet up a tree, sledding down hills that should have been reserved as double-black-diamond ski trails, riding his bike like a trained stuntman. Jim said J.J. had been a total pain in the ass about school, forgetful as shit, the class clown, always in the principal's office.

"I guess nothing ever changes," Nate said. Because J.J. had been the same damn way in the Army, the first one to volunteer to charge into a building they only half believed was abandoned, and most of the time Nate wondered if he would have even remembered his ruck if he hadn't seen Nate hoist his on.

Except, of course, everything *had* changed.

There was a terrible silence, and no one looked at anyone else. Jim's fingers gripped the table.

Then Braden, with the brilliant innocence of childhood, piped up, "Is there any dessert?" and the moment shifted and dissipated, and Suzy brought out the most amazing chocolate cake.

"WELCOME HOME!"

Jake was sitting on the rolling stool in his office, reading patient records. Getting caught up, she assumed. He was tanned and looked even more ridiculously fit than usual. He moved so easily with his prosthesis and was so utterly unconcerned by it that most of the time she completely forgot it existed.

"Thanks," he said, looking up.

"How was Hawaii?"

"Damn nice." A smile spread over his handsome face.

"I'm going to chalk that goofy grin up to your surroundings," she said, grinning back.

"Well, the beaches are lovely. But so was the company."

Alia felt a stab of unexpected envy. After five years of marriage, the two of them were still so happy in each other's company.

She'd never really craved that. At least not before. She'd been content with the idea of having a life of meaning. With taking away people's pain.

"How'd it go here while I was gone?"

"It was great. The movement therapy class is up to six regulars, and—"

"I heard you did morning meditation." He raised his eyebrows. "That was gutsy. Plus, I had three different men tell me they would just as soon I go back to Hawaii so you could keep laying hands on them. And I stopped in to see Nate this morning and he looked almost like his old self. You must have done some kind of magic on him."

She winced. She hadn't seen Nate since the other day at the lake. She'd wondered, even, if he'd left—but apparently not. She couldn't figure out from the butterflies in her stomach whether that was good or bad news.

"Not magic. He still has a lot of pain."

"But he says he's feeling much more in control of it. Not blindsided nearly as often, more able to find strategies to work with it."

"That's good news. I'm glad to hear he's feeling like there's progress."

"He said it was your doing."

She scoffed. "Not if he was looking good this morning—I haven't worked with him in days. I think so much of it is being in a place like this, with other guys who understand what he's been through. Being active, being purposeful. You're doing such a great thing here. I don't think I can take much credit for Nate's progress."

"Well, he feels like you can. And I feel like you can. He's not the only one who swears by what you're doing. I knew I was making a good choice, asking you to come here."

He was making it savagely difficult for her to tell him what she needed to tell him, but she wasn't going to shy from it. If she was going to work here, this was her chance to clear the air.

"Jake."

He must have heard the edge in her tone, because he squared his shoulders like a man taking bad news on the chin.

"I need you to pick up Nate as your client. I need to—recuse myself."

Jake's gaze probed her face for more information, and she found herself, unexpectedly, blushing. Which wasn't lost on Jake. "Did something happen?"

"He—" It wasn't getting any easier to say it. "He kissed me."

"Oh, shit." Jake's eyes widened.

"Yeah." She couldn't quite look at him.

"What happened?"

So much for not too much detail.

"We were swimming and we were on the other side of the lake, and he had pain, and I tried to help, and then—" She peeked. He looked pretty horrified, which she couldn't blame him for. "I know. I should haven't touched him out of the context of the office, but I ran into him swimming across the lake, and he was struggling, and I was worried about him making it back across the lake, so I tried to do some tapping and massage—"

He didn't say anything, only crossed his arms and fixed her with a hard look.

"I know. I know." She wasn't going to let herself think about how far she'd let things go before she'd rebuffed Nate. Her brain had shut down. Her body had taken over. But as soon as she'd recovered her senses . . . "It won't happen again. I made that completely clear. I explained how the rules work, that I couldn't be involved with him if I was treating him."

"Oh, hell," said Jake, running his hand through his hair. "See, this is the downside of having a female therapist in an army of sex-deprived men. I've got friends who own retreats who won't even hire women, and of course I was like, bullshit, that's wrong, that's illegal, I'm not going to do that, but damn. You can see why it's tempting to go that route."

She shook her head. "No. That's not the right answer, and you know it. And this won't be a problem. We'll transfer his care to you. Everything will be fine. *I want this job.* I can handle this situation. Whatever it takes. Look at it this way: Now you know that if a conflict of interest arises, I can handle it in an aboveboard way."

He paced back and forth a few times along the length of the office, finally settled with his hands on the windowsill, facing away from her. "Okay," he said. "Okay. You're right. And I feel bad, too. I'm partially to blame. I shouldn't have let you treat him in the first place." He turned to her, his face lined with concern. "So, okay, let's do this. I'll take over his care. And what's going to happen between you and Nate?"

"Nothing. I'm not going to let sex get in the way of working for R-and-R."

"And that's all it is? Sexual attraction on his part? You're not interested in something more with him?"

She shook her head. It wasn't so much that she wasn't interested, but that she couldn't imagine a positive outcome for anything between them.

"Because even if you're not treating him—" He hesitated, shook his head. "It's none of my business, but you're like a sister to me, and I have some personal experience with this stuff, and I just think it would be a really bad idea to get yourself involved with him."

"I know. That's why nothing's going to happen. I'm not interested in making anything happen. I know a guy in his shoes isn't in a position to—"

She remembered, abruptly, that she was talking about a guy like the guy that Jake had once been, not very long ago, and shut her mouth fast.

Jake frowned, but Alia was pretty sure he wasn't angry. "He's vulnerable. I've been there. Trying to put your life back together when your body isn't what it used to be—and with the painkiller issue on top of that. But I've got to tell you, you're vulnerable, too. Some PTs get to like it a little too much, healing people. It's a powerful thing, stopping someone's pain."

"I know." It *was* a powerful thing. Nate's face, smoothed suddenly of pain lines. How close his expression was to bliss, how much removing pain felt like giving pleasure, so seductive. It had definitely been part of what had propelled her yesterday, stripped away her good judgment. And she knew, too, how easily Nate could mistake the sudden cessation of pain for gratification.

"It's not a good basis for any kind of relationship."

"I know," she repeated.

"I know you know. I'm trying—I want you here. I want you here, and happy, and not all wrapped up in Nate's . . . stuff."

"I'm not—or I won't be, once you start treating him."

"Look. We talked about this at the beginning. How hard it is to keep your distance."

"I fell down on that." Her only hope, she knew, was to totally own it. "But I swear this had way, way more to do with having a history with Nate than with anything else. There is no way I am going to have trouble keeping my distance with any other client, Jake. I promise. Swear to God."

"If I'd been here, you would have come talk to me right away, right? Before—"

"Absolutely."

Jake sighed. "Alia, I really want to give you this job."

"I really want you to give me this job."

He stared at her long and hard, as if trying to reassure himself of something, then nodded. "Okay. Okay. I'm going to dig around in the couch cushions. I don't know where the money's going to come from, but I'll figure it out. Just give me a little more time, okay? In the meantime, can you stay on and help with my schedule? If you take on a few more of my clients, I can call some potential donors. I can't promise it will lead to a job, but I will do my damnedest."

"I wouldn't need a huge salary."

He looked down his nose at her. "That's the shittiest

salary negotiation I've ever heard. But thanks. I'll do my best. I want you to be happy here, and getting paid fairly is a big part of that. And room and board. And benefits."

"I really love it here." It was true, quite apart from how loose and limber, how strangely peaceful, touching Nate Riordan had made her feel. She loved the woods, the lake, the no-nonsense male energy—even the terrible stories and sometimes disturbing volatility of the veterans. "It's the first time I've ever felt like I was really using all my—" She stopped.

"Gifts," finished Jake, the soft word odd, coming from such a tough guy, but she knew it was the way she would have finished the sentence if she'd had the nerve.

"They need me," she said quietly.

"Yes," he said, his gaze on her face thoughtful. "They do."

11

Nate stared at the text he'd written for a moment before he hit send.

You ditched me!

He hoped she'd take it in the spirit in which it was intended. He wasn't mad. Okay, maybe he was a little mad. Because she'd said if he laid off the kissing, she'd still be able to treat him, but then she'd gone and—dumped him. On Jake. If she was going to do that, why not give in to temptation? Why not let the intense chemistry play out?

When Jake broke the news that Alia was turning his treatment over, he'd had about ten thousand different emotions in an instant. A sense of betrayal—she'd talked to Jake about what had happened—followed by disappointment—she wasn't going to touch him again the way she had those times on the table and beside the lake—followed by relief—well, then! If she wasn't his therapist anymore, he had some other ideas about what they could do instead.

Alia: *How'd you get my cell number?*

Nate: *Your friend. Gabi?*

Alia: *She shouldn't have given it to you.*

Nate: *I can be very charming.*

There was a long silence, during which the phone told him that she was typing and erasing and typing and erasing and typing and—

Alia: *I didn't *ditch* you. You're in competent hands.*

Man, how he *wished.* He couldn't believe she'd served him up that softball.

Nate: *I liked your hands better.*

On the plus side, Jake's hands were twenty percent bigger, at least, and definitely stronger, than Alia's. On the minus side—

Well, he *wasn't Alia.* And Nate didn't mean that in the most obvious of ways. Jake was a skilled healer, no doubt, but this morning Nate had been on the massage table for twenty minutes and he'd still been able to feel nerve pain radiating from that stuck spot behind his shoulder out to his fingertips. Alia wouldn't have let that last more than thirty seconds. She would have used her weird X-ray vision, figured out exactly where it hurt, and extinguished the pain.

"Alia does this tapping thing? Like—" Nate demonstrated to Jake.

"Like this?"

"Um. More like—" Nate showed him the rhythm and the intensity, and Jake dutifully imitated.

Nate sighed. So did Jake. "You know," Jake said mildly, "if you hadn't kissed her, *she* could be doing this right now."

"None of your fucking business, man."

"Oh, there you're wrong. There you're very, very wrong. She is absolutely my business, quite literally. Although frankly, it's not her I'm worried about. It's you. I've been where you are. You're trying to fill gaps, you're trying to prove your body can still do something it used to be able to do—"

Nate threw off Jake's hands and sat up. "Shove it. I'm not paying you to psychoanalyze me."

"Whoa," Jake said, putting his hand on Nate's arm. "I'm not psychoanalyzing you. I'm telling you how it was for me. *I* was trying to fill gaps. *I* was trying to figure out what I was doing and what it meant. *I* was trying to prove my body could still do what it used to be able to do. And I'm just saying, don't do anything stupid. Don't do anything you'll regret. Don't do anything with strings attached you can't afford to play out. That's what I'm saying. What I'm saying is, *Leave her alone.* She wants a job here, and she doesn't need you messing with her head."

"Noted," said Nate tightly.

Only he really must not have noted it very well. Because what was he doing now? He was flirting with Alia.

There were two opposing parts of him. The part that wanted to respect what she wanted, and the part that just *wanted her.*

Alia: *I'll sit down with Jake and make sure he knows what I know.*

Okay. She was trying to keep this in the clean realm.

She doesn't need you messing with her head.

But he wanted to know. He wanted to *know* whether she was *MenInUni242.* Whether she'd been typing, whether she'd been feeding him what she thought he wanted to hear from Becca, or whether she'd been telling him—

Telling him what *she wanted.*

Was it messing with her head to try to find out? Would he be messing with her head any worse than she'd messed with his? He felt like he had a right to know what she'd really been thinking, how she'd felt about him, during that mad period of correspondence and care packages and instant messages.

Nate: *They still won't be your hands.*

There was a long silence. Long enough that he figured she'd decided to ignore him. Which, frankly, he had to admit, was probably what she *should* be doing. Not taking the bait he'd served up, because Jake was way too right about where Nate was coming from and about why sex wasn't just sex in this situation.

He went and found Griff, dragged him out to the archery range. He'd never done archery before R&R, but he was hooked. Loved the feel of the arrow between his fingers, the sensation of pulling the string taut, sighting over his hand, the moment of decision just before release.

Sounded like sex, somehow. Fuck it. Everything sounded like sex to him right now. He couldn't get her out of his head.

Griff loosed an arrow, which lodged itself in the center of the target with a sharp thwack. "Where will you go after you leave here?"

Nate nocked his own arrow. "A friend's parents own a hardware store in southern Oregon." The lack of past tense in that sentence struck him. Should have been a *late* friend or something, but real people didn't say that. He was a dead friend, but no one said that, either. Just a friend. A ghost, of sorts.

"Thought you were a college boy. College degree? Army pedigree? You could do anything."

"I owe him one." Nate buried the arrow in the outermost ring of the target. He frowned. Sad that a guy who could shoot a rifle with so much accuracy was such a miserable mofo with a bow and arrow.

"Your friend—he still in the sandbox?" Griff tilted his head to one side.

Nate shook his head. "Dead."

"So the hardware store—one of those fucking promises, huh?"

"I guess."

"Blame yourself?"

"I guess."

"Everyone does. Like that story you told, about Turk. No one thinks there was anything Turk woulda coulda shoulda done different, but that's not how Turk sees it."

Nate's shoulders were starting to stiffen up, and he knew what Alia would say. That it was about J.J. But maybe she'd be wrong in this case. Maybe it was just about how different this kind of shooting felt from anything else he'd ever done. She couldn't be right about every-fucking-thing.

He and Griff finished up and he was heading back to his room when her text came through.

Alia: *I can't do this.*

Nate: *Do what?*

And then, when radio silence stretched too long, and he couldn't keep himself from filling it: *Yes, you can. I'm not your client anymore. We're just two people.*

Alia: *We're not just two people.*

What did she mean by that? Was she implying that their history meant something, that their history made them more than two bodies gravitationally drawn together?

Alia: *You're a recovering addict. Looking for another fix.*

Oh. Ow.

Harsh. But not unexpected, and not entirely wrong.

It was pretty much what Jake had told him this morning. A little rawer, a little more frank, but a variation on the same theme. He was in no position to start something. He should pocket the goddamn phone before she told him more truth about himself.

Instead, he texted: *And what about you?*

Another one of those long silences. He could imagine her, clutching the phone. Setting it down. Wanting to walk away from what he was asking her.

And then: *What about me?*

Nate: *What are you looking for?*

This time, there was no answer.

She caught herself watching him a million times a day.

She'd taken what was supposed to be a quiet, contemplative, head-clearing walk, and as she'd exited the pasture and stepped out of the first stand of trees, there he was on the archery range with Griff.

She dropped back behind a tree and watched him, appalled at herself for both the spying and the craving that had prompted it.

I liked your hands better.

They still won't be your hands.

And what about you? What are you looking for?

Damn him.

She'd done exactly the right thing and it felt all wrong. Because all she wanted was to give him what he was asking for. Her hands. She wanted to make him feel whatever Jake couldn't. She wanted to make him feel what that look at the lake had begged for the other day.

So maybe she was looking for her next fix, too. And that's why she was hiding behind a tree and watching him.

He was in some kind of super-engaging conversation with Griff, his face all alight with whatever they were talking about.

He wore a pair of well-worn jeans and a form-fitting black T-shirt. That's what he'd worn at the picnic where she'd first seen him. Then, the jeans had been snug over his magnificent ass, and the shirt had strained alarmingly over his chest and biceps. Today he was leaner, but no less eye-catching.

There was something primitively satisfying about watching him shoot, too. Sure, he wasn't bringing down a buffalo for her and their small family of kids, but he *could* have been. Maybe it was that she now knew exactly what those hands could do, and watching them at work, the way those two fingers crooked around the arrow's shaft—

Well, damn.

She snuck away.

The next afternoon, she saw him and one of his other friends—Tron, she thought—down at the lake's edge, skipping stones. They were both big, good-looking guys, but Nate had a grace that echoed the stone's dance over the taut surface of the water. She didn't think he would have been able to whip his arm like that a week ago, not without pain. But he was laughing and joking, and he chucked probably twenty stones while she watched, before he rubbed his shoulder and called it quits.

She could have gone down to the water's edge and skipped with them—she was good at it, could get a stone to bounce six or seven times—but she didn't. She would have wanted to help him with the locked-up shoulder. She would have wanted to lean in close to him and rest her head against his chest. She would have wanted to tilt her face up to his.

And that couldn't happen.

That night at dinner, she saw him in the dining hall, joking and laughing again, making the other guys laugh. There was no doubt that Nate was the kind of guy whose attitude was contagious. A natural-born leader. The guys he'd befriended were all doing better than they'd been doing two weeks ago, making a ton of progress on their rehab and starting to lose that air of darkness they'd had when they arrived.

Maybe Nate had been in a dark place, but he wasn't a dark person. The glow of his old power was surfacing, struggling to shine through fatigue and despair and pain.

"Who are you staring at like you want to eat him for dinner?"

"No one."

"Don't tell me 'no one,'" Gabi said. "You're drooling."

Alia frowned. "No one. I swear."

Gabi leaned in confidentially. "I know the rules. We all know the rules. I'm married, for God's sake. But it doesn't hurt to look. Just tell me, who's got you so distracted the fork's missing your mouth?"

Gabi was right. It didn't hurt to look. "Black T-shirt."

"Niiiiiiice."

"It's kind of a bummer, though," Melinda said thoughtfully. "So many men, so much muscle, so much testosterone, and all off-limits."

Alia watched Nate slug Griff in the shoulder, deliver some

kind of punch line with his index finger extended, then grab his plate and bus it. And there it was. Man, muscle, testosterone, doing its work on her body and emotions. A held-back smile in her chest, heat pooling between her legs, and something in her reaching out for him.

She really needed to get out of here before she found herself walking in his direction.

She got up so abruptly she almost knocked her chair over.

"Whoa, baby," Melinda said, laughing.

"I think I'm gonna take it easy tonight. Read in bed, fall asleep early."

Gabi sighed. "Sounds nice. I've got to pull together snacks for movie night tonight."

"Could be fun."

"Could be," Gabi said. "Would be *more* fun if I were in your shoes, drooling over one of them and at least getting to *fantasize* it could happen, instead of going home to my deadbeat husband who will probably be farting and snoring when I crawl into bed."

"At least he's a sure thing," Alia offered.

"Not if he's been out drinking," Gabi said, and sighed.

Alia gave her a sympathetic look, said good night to her friends, picked up her tray, and headed back to her room.

She changed into pajamas, brushed her teeth, and crawled into bed. The rooms in the main building, where both she and Nate were housed, were not quite as well appointed as typical business-hotel rooms, but they had their own bathrooms, and if they were spare in décor and amenities, they were clean and bright.

She reached out her hand. Touched her cellphone. It would be so easy. She'd done it once before.

I want your tongue all over me.

I want you to pin me down.

I want your cock in my mouth. As much as I can hold.

Those instant messages that for nearly two years she'd wished she'd never written. But now?

What she'd done had been absolutely, one hundred percent wrong, and yet—

She slid a hand into the waistband of her pajama pants, touched herself where she was already aching for him. Bodies didn't lie. When she'd sent those texts?

She'd meant them. Absolutely, one hundred percent.

She had her phone cradled in her palm now, her thumb moving restlessly just over the place where swiping would bring the screen alive.

Quite apart from the job, quite apart from her promises to Jake, there was the reality of Nate's situation. Of *their* situation. That he had nothing to give, and that her own motives for wanting to help him were tangled and dark. That it gave her a rush to know he needed her. *Wanted her.*

And it only made it hotter that the way he wanted her wasn't pure, either.

She set the phone on the floor. Pushed it as hard as she could, so it slid across the floor and bumped to a rest against the opposite wall.

There.

Safe.

12

She was awakened in the pitch dark by knocking at her door.

Her nervous system went nuts—heart pounding, breath rapid—until she realized it was only eleven—not obscenely late. Maybe Gabi stopping by after the movie for girl talk? She roused herself and went groggily to the door, peered out through the peephole.

At first she didn't see him, because he was leaning his head against the door. She opened it very slowly so she wouldn't hurt him. "I'm sorry," he whispered roughly.

"You shouldn't be here." But there was no force behind her words. Because he was in pain, and he'd come to her, and both of them knew she wouldn't turn him away.

He raised his head and took her in. For the first time in her life, she wished her pajama style ran more toward Victoria's Secret and less toward worn T-shirt and flannel pants.

Even though she shouldn't have wished that, because she was supposed to be making sure nothing else happened between them.

And not that it would have mattered to him if she'd been wearing black lace. He was deep in his suffering. When she stepped back to let him in, he moved past her like a zombie and crumpled into her desk chair.

She turned the desk lamp on because it was the least glaring and closed the door.

She knew she should make him go downstairs to her office. She'd made this mistake once before, and she'd outright promised Jake she'd learned from her error. And while even her office wasn't a completely safe place to be with him at eleven o'clock at night, at least it would provide the semblance of professionalism. Here—

Here, they were in her bedroom. She was in her pajamas.

"Nate, I can't—"

"Please."

"You should go."

He raised his head and let her see his eyes. Dark, pained, craving. "I need your hands on me."

There were a thousand other ways he could have asked her, a thousand missteps that might have allowed her to summon the self-control to send him away, but he'd said that instead. She felt it, straight to her core, her blood heating everywhere.

She took a deep breath.

"Lie down," she said. "On your stomach."

She crossed the room, stood beside the bed.

She began as she would have begun in her office. Because maybe there was still hope that if she kept this official, professional, it wouldn't go where she hoped it wouldn't and prayed it would.

The bed was entirely the wrong height, impossible. So

she pulled over a chair and tried to work from it, but the angle was difficult and her own body began to protest. Then she tried sitting at the edge of the bed, which felt risky but not terrifying. But that was awkward, too, twisted. For tapping it wasn't so bad, but when she wanted to put pressure somewhere, when she wanted to lean in, it was uncomfortable.

She was about to tell him it wouldn't work. She was about to say—God's truth—that years ago she'd promised herself she wouldn't work in a way that put her body at risk. That put her career at risk.

But then he made a sound. Not a sensual sound. A hurt sound, part grunt, part groan, part whimper.

There was probably something wrong with her, because she felt that sound not only in the parts of her that were primed for care, but in the secret, hungry parts, too. His wordless plea for help felt like sex.

She didn't have any more resistance, not for any of the things he made her want.

She climbed onto the bed, onto him, and she felt him go rigid for a moment and then relax. This was what she'd wanted all along, to be able to comfort him with her whole body, however it was needed. She gave in to it and lay down along his back, pressing her check to the groove at the base of his neck, letting her hands reach around to cup the caps of his shoulders. She was hyperaware of her breasts against his back, and he must have been, too, because he groaned, and it wasn't a groan of pain. And beneath her hips, she felt him move ever-so-slightly, pressing into the bed.

Her body reacted like a shot, molten heat pouring down deep.

What the *hell* was she doing?

She raised her head. She couldn't. Of course she couldn't. She started to sit up—

"No," he said quickly. "Don't move. Please. You're helping."

"Nate—"

"Please."

It was less a plea than a command. He reached a hand back and grabbed her thigh, but then he made a sound that was definitely pain, twisted and harsh. The sound called out to that part of her that couldn't refuse him, and after a moment she lowered herself again. Tried to tell his body, with hers, to let go.

"What were you doing?" she asked after a moment.

"When?"

"When the pain started?"

"I was in bed. Just lying there."

"What were you thinking about?"

"What does it matter?"

"It matters." Just as it mattered that all she could think about was how much better she could make him feel if there were no layers of clothing between them. If it were only her skin and his.

He was silent, under her.

"J.J.? The tower?"

He didn't answer, so she knew she was right. "It's. Not. In. My. Fucking. Head."

"I know." She touched him now, pushing his shirt up, taking unabashed pleasure in the heat of his back, the glide of her hands over his warm skin, the messages his body sent to hers through her fingertips and palms, up her arms, into her nipples. From the hard curve of his ass between her thighs, the almost-contact of those muscles against the aching vee of her sex.

He moved again beneath her. Rocking against the bed. So slightly that if she weren't so attuned to every shift of his skin and muscle, she might have missed it. And without making a conscious decision to do it, she tilted her hips down against him, pressing him to the mattress. Again, her thighs clenching, her body tightening against the perfect pressure of his glutes, so the pull and stretch almost made her go out of her mind.

For a moment, she let herself think it, fully. To imagine exactly what she wanted to do most, to rock and press him into the bed, again and again, until he found his release. That total unlocking, pain and holding flying apart into pure pleasure, that surge of heat and light that was oxytocin flowing free through his bloodstream. She could feel it, as if it were hers. That was how much she wanted to give it to him. How much she wanted him to have it.

And they could almost pretend that it wasn't happening. That her body solid against his from behind was part of something else, some act of nurture, even as both of them were completely aware of his cock, hard underneath him. Even as they both egged him on, her hips against his ass, his cock throbbing against the resistance of the bed, the skin stretching over the swollen head—

Whether consciously or unconsciously, his hips had found a rhythm against her bed, under her, and he clutched a handful of her pillow in his fist. As her hands moved over his body, she felt another wash of liquid heat. In a moment she'd soak through the layers between them.

His hips sped up beneath her.

"Li."

It was a groan. Now absolutely a plea.

Her name broke the spell. His acknowledgment that he knew, that he was here, too. That there was no pretending.

She was flooded with shame.

She untangled herself, climbed off him.

"Li—"

But she wouldn't let him talk, wouldn't let him say whatever he was going to say to her. She sat on the edge of the bed and she made her words take up all the space in the room so neither of them could acknowledge what had almost happened. "The pain's not in your head. It's in your body. But your head keeps sending your body pain messages. And I think I know what might help. You trust me, right? You trust me?"

Of course, she knew the answer to his question long before the words came out of his mouth. Even though he shouldn't trust her. Even though she was betraying the trust Jake had placed in her, by being here, but way beyond that, by letting herself take what wasn't hers to take.

Even though she didn't trust herself. Not at all.

"I'm here, aren't I?"

13

The way he wanted her crowded out pain. Obliterated it.

What was it about her? That she could make a T-shirt and pajama pants look like something out of a porn flick? The flush of sleep in her cheeks, the tousled bed-head of hair, the fuck-me sag of her bottom lip, none of which was remotely intentional?

No. More likely, the way she'd opened the door and stepped back to let him in, even though they both knew what she was sacrificing. The way she moved in the room, businesslike, doing what had to be done. A glimpse of what she would be like taking care of people in the middle of the night, a family, a household.

The way she'd told him to lie down. The way she'd climbed on top of him. The way she'd moved against him, picking up his rhythm, so she was fucking him and he was fucking the bed, and he'd never been so turned on in his life. Like he could lift and throw a truck, though what he'd rather do was flip her off him and cover her body with his and crush her mouth until she whimpered.

Did he trust her? It was a ridiculous question. He would let her do anything to him, and he would ask her to let him do everything he wanted to her.

Mostly, though, he wanted her to finish what she'd started. His cock was so hard, his balls drawn up so tight to his body, that they ached. And he felt he was on the brink of something life-changing, because the woman who had climbed on top of him, who had tilted her hips down, was familiar—

MenInUni242, is that you?

Except now she was all business again.

"I want to try something."

As if they could forget the weight and heat of her on him. The way they'd found a rhythm together. How close they'd come to chasing it home.

He snorted. "I want to try something, too."

"Not that." She crossed her arms, ruining the view.

"Yes, that. Get back here. Alia. Seriously. Don't try to play like you weren't—"

Instead, she stepped away and sat in the desk chair. Her nipples poked through the thin fabric of her T-shirt. He rolled onto his side and winced as pain shot up his back and spiraled in his neck.

"See, you're in no condition for *that*."

"I'm in perfect condition for that," he said, indicating the steel rod in his athletic pants.

Her gaze flicked to his groin, then away. Then her eyes met his. There was a challenge in them. "I want you to meditate."

"Not that again."

"Yes, that, again."

"I have a better idea," he said. "I think you should meditate. You can use this as a focal point." He dropped his palm to where his cock was distending his pants, and ground his hand there. It was only the barest relief. There wasn't going to be any relief for him until he was buried in her, and then— then he bet he'd be ready for her again ten minutes after they were done.

She was staring at the slow rock and squeeze of his hand, her face soft and intense. Her fingers twitched against her flannel-clad thigh. Her tongue came out to wet her lips. *Bingo.*

He elaborated, a slow drawl, his eyes on her face the whole time, watching the effect of his words. "I want you to focus on it and make it the sole object in your mind. I want you to consider all its aspects thoroughly until you reach enlightenment. Or I do. Whichever comes first. I'm all for both."

She giggled.

"Did you just laugh at me?"

"Were you expecting something else?" Now she met his eyes.

"Admit it, you're tempted."

She shook her head. "Nate, stop."

But he wouldn't let her gaze go, and the flush got deeper in her cheeks, until she shook her head and said, "I admit it. Now be quiet. And listen to me."

He sucked his breath in. "God, I love a bossy woman."

In fact, he wasn't sure what had gotten to him most, her bossing him or the giggle, which was so unlike her, or her outright admission that she wanted him. Whatever it was, it had him going, bad. Bad enough to want to mess with her. To get lust to win out over shame in her, to get her to finish what she'd started. What she'd promised with those hips and the press of her breasts against his back and the feel of her breath on his neck. The shift and acceleration of her breathing.

"Aaaaand. Now I don't think I'm going to be able to meditate. Don't I have to concentrate on something? If it's something other than your nipples, I'm probably SOL."

He knew he was pushing his luck, but something—the color of her cheeks, the hugeness of her pupils, the way she couldn't look away—told him that his strategy was working.

MenInUni242 would like it this way. The banter. The alpha. The badness. The outright *sex* of it.

"You're supposed to focus on your breath," she said dryly.

"I could focus on *your* breath. I could focus on making you pant like a dog."

"Nate, shut *up*." But she was laughing. And her eyes were so warm, he could drown in them. "Just try this for me, okay?"

He got up and started to cross to her, but she nailed him with her gaze. "Sit. Down."

He sat.

"Lie down."

He obeyed. "I had no idea how dom you could be."

"Close your eyes."

"Are you going to tie me up?"

He heard her cross the room, and then she was kneeling beside him, her breath on his cheek as she whispered, "I know this freaks you out. I totally get it. But just . . . just try it, okay?"

Such a girl thing to say—*I know this freaks you out*—and

usually he hated that kind of shit, that *I know you better than you know yourself* bullshit, but the thing was, she kind of did. At least when it came to pain, she was the expert.

"Take a few deep breaths."

He was so tempted to turn his head and take her mouth, but instead he did what she'd asked.

"Relax your whole body."

I can't relax my whole *body, sweetheart. Not while you're that close to me.* But he didn't say it out loud. Because he was willing to try this. For *her.* He was pretty sure there was no one else on earth he would have done it for.

"Pay attention to your breath. Just follow it. In, out—"

"Better stop that, babe."

"In . . . out . . ."

She was stubborn. Or maybe she was doing it on purpose to be provocative. Either way, he liked it.

"Just notice the breath. Don't try to control it."

It was surprisingly relaxing. The pain was still niggling in his neck and shoulder, but it wasn't as bad as it had been.

As he was about to drift off to sleep, he heard her voice, soft and husky. "Now choose a spot in your body where there's pain. Focus on that spot."

He shook his head. "I don't want to *focus* on my pain."

"Just do it." He couldn't tell if she was amused or exasperated.

"Tyrant," he muttered, but he obeyed. Ah, shit, that *hurt.* Teasing her, joking with her, having her body all over his— those had been great distractions, but now here he was, focusing, and *fuck.*

"Observe the pain."

As if he had a choice.

"Notice whether it's hot, or cold . . ."

Hot. Like something had seared him. But there were places where it felt cold, too. *Huh.*

"Whether it's buzzing or burning or twisting . . ."

Part of his brain was resisting her—*Fuck this. It's pain. I don't give a shit if it buzzes or burns or twists*—but the part that was going along with her was intrigued. Now twisting. Now almost—shuddering. Now sharp, then suddenly much duller. Now—

"Notice if it's steady or if it comes and goes."

Where had it gone? Oh, there it was again—and now gone.

So it wasn't a steady thing. It was a thing that came and —*Fuck.* He dug his fists into the bed.

"Try not to fight it. Try to *accept* it."

"You fucking accept it."

"I can't do this for you."

She was so stolid. A wall of determination.

He tried. To accept it.

"*Yes, pain.* Say it. In your head. Yes, pain."

"No—"

"Try it."

Yes, pain.

It ebbed. Just a little. Surprised, he drew his first full breath in several minutes.

"If it becomes too much, notice another part of your body that isn't in pain. Like your feet, or your hands—"

Or my cock—huh. Not hard anymore. He'd been concentrating so intently on his pain that he'd forgotten that Alia was still practically in the bed with him. And now he'd unforgotten. He could smell her shampoo. Something that was probably deodorant. And that deep-down, sweet sex smell. *Damn.* He wanted to bury his face between her legs and—

"And if something takes your attention away from the pain"—so she'd spotted the fact that his attention had wandered, huh?—"notice that, and then come back to the pain. Try to relax all your physical muscles around the pain—"

Physical muscles? That was redundant.

"And all the mental muscles you're clenching around the pain, one at a time—"

Huh. Mental muscles. She was a quack. She was just a quack, and this was bullshit, and he was going to get up from the bed in about three seconds and back her up against a wall because it was going to be *his* turn to tell her what to do, and he wasn't going to waste any more time on hokey bullshit voodoo.

"And all the emotional muscles you're clenching around the pain."

All at once, he got what she meant. There was a kind of holding in his chest, and he *could* let it out, like a breath. It felt like a flower unfolding, one petal at a time. Because right here, here was how badly he craved one of those little white pills he'd flushed down the toilet. And right here, here was how scared he'd been ninety percent of the time in Afghanistan, and the time he'd felt safest had been the time he'd been least safe. And right here? How much he wanted one more chance to give J.J. shit. And how goddamn much it sucked that Braden couldn't go on a fucking kayaking trip with his fucking father and had to accept Nate as a shitty substitute—

"It's okay," she was saying.

A tear slid down the side of his face into his ear. That wasn't *his*, was it? In his chest, something was thawing and breaking up like an iceberg. *Oh, fuck, no. No fucking way.* He swiped the back of his hand across his eyes.

"Accept whatever comes up. Say *yes* to it."

"Shut up. Shut *up.*"

"Yes, anger. Yes, grief."

"Shut *up,* Alia."

"Yes, to whatever is there—"

"Alia!" He sat up and grabbed her arms, shook her. "Shut the fuck up and get up here and let me kiss you. Okay? That's all. That's what I say yes to. Just—just—"

Then she was in his arms and her mouth was on his and *yes,* this.

14

His hands were in her hair, and not only to brace her so he could pelt her mouth with kisses, but raking through her hair and pulling it and stroking it, like he couldn't decide whether he wanted to pet her or hurt her.

That was fine, because after all this time of holding herself back, of treating him and caring for him, she was done. She was done with gentle and thoughtful and nurturing. She was giving as good as she got, grabbing handfuls of whatever she could, learning his body in this new and different and totally satisfying way. The shift of muscle against her taut nipples, against the greedy heat between her legs, against the cling of her thighs as she tried to pin and contain and define him. *Mine.*

Making up, somehow, for her failure to lay claim to him the first time she'd ever seen him, when she could have told Becca, *Yes, I met him first.*

He had this way of kissing. Short, greedy kisses, like he was desperate to get more of her but couldn't make himself be patient enough to get what he needed. It drove her crazy. It made her kiss back with raw hunger, a craving that rose up from the core of her being, more primitive, even, than the roar of arousal between her legs.

The tempo shifted abruptly and his kisses became long and sweet and deep, his tongue sweeping in and claiming her. She'd thought that when he kissed her like that, like he meant it, like he was stopping to savor, she'd feel a sense of relief, but all she felt was a doubling and redoubling of the hunger. Her hands went off on a spree, yanking and squeezing and pinching, and he yelped because she'd bitten the heck out of his lower lip. "Do that again," he ordered.

She was pure, naked id now. She clenched his thigh between hers so she could rub her achy sex up and down the hard muscle, whimpering his name, clutching his head so she could get more of his mouth. And she didn't care how needy, how pathetic, how desperate she looked or sounded, because he was doing the same thing. He was saying her name over and over, a murmured mantra, bucking and thrusting against whatever he could get purchase on, and there was no rhyme nor reason to the way his hands roamed —not to give her pleasure, but out of control, territorial, possessive. Because *he* needed.

"You," he said and groaned. "Oh, God. You. Are. A. Goddess."

He crawled over her and trapped her between his arms and legs, and lowered himself onto her. Then slowly, so slowly it was a form of delicious torture, he lightly rubbed his cotton-clad erection against the seam of her pajama pants. One layer of fabric communicated friction to the other, and it resonated in her sex, just enough vibration to be felt but not enough to relieve the building tension.

Back and forth, a little harder now, and he braced up on both arms, muscles lengthening and bunching, powerful and male. It was almost too much, the sight of him over her, the sensation mounting between her legs, the look on his face, because he was feeling it, too, that same friction, and she could almost see it gathering behind his eyes as they locked on hers. So intense, that locked gaze, so intimate, like he knew how her body was tightening down around his touch, like he could see the exact shape and size of her hunger.

And then more pressure, a little of his weight now, and she moaned and licked her lips.

He made a noise that had no translatable name and dropped his head to kiss her. The long, deep, possessive kind. She wasn't sure if it was deliberate or whether he'd half forgotten what he was doing, but he'd pressed his hips to hers fully now and was grinding against her.

"Nate." Into his mouth. And then, turning her head to break away, "Nate, ease up, or I'm going to come—"

He raised himself up and gave her a wicked look, then locked his gaze on hers again and thrust against her, and where all the tension had bundled itself together and was poised and waiting, something gave suddenly, a lost hold on control, the first breath after rising through layers of water, a vast lever under weight and strain, and her orgasm surged up and broke over her in wave after wave after wave.

INSTINCT DROVE HIM. He was frantic in a way he couldn't remember ever having been with any other woman. The ache in his cock and balls, worse now that he'd partially whetted it by stroking himself over her, worse now that he'd watched that orgasm rise, color in her throat and face, lust like panic in her eyes.

If he didn't watch himself he'd rub himself off on her in two more strokes and it would be over. And he—he didn't know if he'd get a second chance.

He rolled away from her, hating the loss of contact, but bent on something better. What it would be like to watch her come again, *feel* her this time, to be buried as deep as he could get inside her.

"Condoms. Alia. Where?"

"Bathroom cabinet."

He crossed to the bathroom and found the condoms. "This box is *waaaay* too small," he informed her.

Her lips curved. Her lids were heavy, her face soft with pleasure. God, she turned him on. He couldn't get his clothes off fast enough. He pulled roughly, his movements jerky. She was laughing at him. But she stopped laughing when he got his shirt over his head and kicked his jeans down. She wasn't laughing at all. He loved the look in her eyes. Covetous. He could feel that look like a touch, smoothing warmth over his chest, drifting down his belly to the waistband of his boxer briefs. Wanting *in,* the way he wanted into her. He'd let her look all day if she wanted. He'd known—no, he'd *hoped*— she'd look like that. Like a woman who knew exactly what she was asking for.

He held himself in one hand, freed himself with the other, pushing his briefs down, and he watched her eyes and her mouth. Eyes getting darker, bigger, sleepier, mouth softening a little, and then he saw the tip of her tongue and he thought of *MenInUni242* saying, *I want your cock in my mouth. As much as I can hold.* And he almost asked her. *Do you?* But what if she didn't? That would bring this to a screeching halt as she realized that he'd been fantasizing about someone else. Someone they both knew wasn't Becca but maybe wasn't Alia, either.

So he didn't say it. But he thought it, and he got that much harder, dreaming that she did want his cock in her mouth, as much as she could hold, that she'd suck him to the back of her throat and—

Nope, unless he was going to ruin this gig in the most unmanly of ways. Couldn't think like that anymore.

So instead he helped her with her clothes, which was as much of a laugh as tearing off his own had been—they kept getting caught and he made faint sounds of frustration and protest, and she giggled and helped, until she was wearing only a pale green pair of lace panties. He wouldn't have figured her for pale green lace. Something as down-to-earth as the rest of her outfit, more like.

God. She was beautiful. Breasts right in that sweet spot between more-than-a-handful and what-the-fuck-do-I-do-with-these? Her nipples pale pink, and a little dip of a navel in the center of a belly that managed to show both ridges of muscle and gentle slope. Strong thighs that had gripped his thigh earlier, his hips, that had generously cushioned his increasingly ragged, out-of-control thrusts. She was like a cross between a Greek statue celebrating the human form and a fertility goddess.

He could see it in her eyes. As much as he loved the way

she'd looked at him, she was getting off now because he couldn't stop staring at her. Lying back, she let him own her with his gaze, and then that *tongue* again, wetting her lips—

Oh, fuck.

She was breathing fast. She reached to push her panties down. Which was good because pretty or no, those panties were between him and what he wanted, which was to feel that softness and that unyieldingness, to get back into that rhythm she'd set for them earlier, because that was the thing that had really gotten to him, because, *fuck,* that had been her, back there, pretending it wasn't happening, even as her body was making it happen. Because she wanted it even more than she thought it was a bad idea.

He slid his thumb along the seam of her sex, parted her curls, and almost lost his shit completely when he felt how wet she was. And how swollen.

He groaned and slid a finger in.

She whimpered.

"Oh, fuck. Alia, I—"

"Condom."

He tore the box, extracted his prize. Ripped the packet, rolled it on. He knew exactly where he wanted to be, and he wanted to get there as quickly as possible. She reached her arms up, opening her mouth, drawing him down to kiss him, lifting her hips, rubbing her wetness on him, and he grabbed his cock to guide himself to her. She was clumsy, too, in her eagerness, pushing back as he was finding her, breaching her, savoring how tight she was, like his fist on a good night, only wet and twice as hot and better, because it was *her,* and he thrust once and then she gripped him tight around the hips and there it was, that rhythm she'd teased him with earlier,

Alia moving against him like there was no way she could resist what her body was demanding—

"I'm sorry, Alia. I will do better some other time," he declared, before he abandoned good sense and all the rules of first-time sex and everything he knew about being a halfway decent lover, and gave up holding back—everything. Gratitude, mostly. Because she could make the pain go away. Because she was ready, willing, and eager. Because she was under him thrusting back as hard as he thrust into her, because for every time he called her name she called his. Because she was coming again, milking him, bending his will and owning him.

Everything in him, physical, mental, emotional, was clenching and unclenching, locked up tighter than a vault and broken wide open, far wider than his known universe. It was only her teeth in his shoulder and her fingernails in his back that kept him anchored to the bed.

15

"**B**etter?" she asked.

He'd collapsed on top of her, his face in her neck, her hair tickling his nose. Barely holding his weight off her. Only a little bit of him still careful and aware. The part that acted now to extricate himself, condom safely stripped away and disposed of. So he could shift again to put his arms around her. So he could sigh into her hair and keep her warm like she'd warmed him earlier this evening.

And then her single word fully penetrated his haze. She was asking if he felt better. As if she'd just administered a session of tapping.

"Pain gone?" she asked, in case he'd somehow missed the significance of her question the first time.

It was. His whole body was bathed in a warm glow, not at all unlike the drug glow he'd craved until a few days ago. All traces of pain had vanished. Although he could feel himself tensing up again already against her questions.

And then he was pissed at himself for being such a girl. What was so bad about her asking him that? What had he expected her to ask him? Whether she'd rocked his world like he'd rocked hers? If it was the best he'd ever had? If he'd like a cigarette?

So he answered her with the truth, or at least the truth he knew she most wanted to hear right then, which was "I needed that." He propped himself up on one elbow and smiled at her.

She looked genuinely pleased to hear it, which went a long way toward tamping down any stray disappointment he felt. So did how happy she looked herself, relaxed and pink-cheeked and red-lipped and just plain beautiful. He bent his head and kissed her, and she kissed him right back, and he realized, because of how strong his relief felt right then, that he'd been waiting for her to freak out. To say, *We can't have done that, we didn't do that, we can't do that again.* And he was not ready to quit her. Not anywhere near yet.

For one thing, that sex had, in fact, rocked his world. A-grade, top-of-the-line, write-home-about-it. You didn't walk away from sex like that, even if things were a little complicated.

And for another, there was still the *MenInUni242* question.

"That felt really good," she said.

"Sorry it was so short-lived. It has . . . been a while." Then he shook his head, because there was too much half-truth already in that room. "Honestly? That's not why. It has been a while, but the thing is—" He made a sheepish face. "I am into you. No. Correction. I am *so* into you."

"Oh." Her face lit with surprise and pleasure, which, damn, felt good.

"So I'm going to lay this out there, and you can feel free to say something that will shred my pride to teeny-tiny threads, but that? From beginning to end? That will go into the private mental porn library, forever and permanently."

"Oh," she said, more distinctly.

"Maybe that's not the most romantic—"

She cut him off. "No. Me, too. In the porn library."

"Really? You mean it?" He was actually a little hung up on the fact that she *had* a private mental porn library, and what its other contents were. Did it bear any resemblance to *MenInUni242*'s?

Suddenly, he had to know. "Alia?"

"Uh-huh?"

"I want to ask you something. Back during the whole thing with Becca, there were these instant messages—"

Her face darkened, and he realized what crappy timing he had. Bringing that whole history into things right now, when they were lying here in the afterglow, very much in the present. What if she thought he was thinking of Becca, at a time like this? He would hate for her to suspect that. When all he could think about was getting into her again.

"I'm sorry. I'm so sorry."

It took him a minute. First to understand what she was apologizing for, and then to grasp the implications.

Hope rose like a balloon. "You wrote them."

"Becca never told you?"

"We never talked about them."

She blinked a few times, then shook her head. "God, Nate. I thought she—I'm so sorry. There's no excuse. I know that. Just, I'm sorry."

His brain couldn't work quite fast enough to keep up with all this. With how guilty she looked and how psyched he was

that she'd typed those words, but also how it didn't neces-
sarily mean what he wanted it to mean. Just because it had
been her fingers on the keyboard didn't mean the fantasies
had sprung from her imagination.

"Did Becca tell you what to write?"

She shook her head, and he felt the knowledge shift and
settle at the base of his spine, in that dark impression where
desire came from. *Those words came from her mind.* And *still,*
he didn't know enough. Whether she'd meant them.
Whether they'd felt like her when she'd written them.
Whether she'd *claim* them now. But now she was looking
away from him, and the plea when it came was barely more
than a whisper.

"Do we have to talk about this?"

Abruptly, he realized it wasn't only guilt she was feeling,
but shame, too.

So either she hadn't meant them or she couldn't own
them.

He could feel the mood shifting, and any moment she was
going to fold under the weight of her old shame, remember
why this escapade could cost her her job. Did it really matter
so much what had happened a year and a half ago, when he
had her here, in her bed, and she was willing and responsive
and—

"It doesn't matter," he said firmly. "It doesn't matter.
Okay?"

"You'd have every right to still be mad. It was a shitty
thing I did."

Ironic. In her mind, having written those dirty words
made her more the bad guy. In his—

Well, it made her the kind of bad girl he still hoped to find when he'd peeled away her inhibitions.

"I know you did it to help Becca."

"That doesn't make it okay."

"It's in the past," he said. Because she was right. It didn't make it okay. But maybe he couldn't be angry at someone who'd made him feel as good as Alia had. Maybe there was a statute of limitations on how long he could care about what he'd lost, when he had her, warm and beautiful, limber and willing, stretched out beside him.

He would probably never know how much of *MenIn-Uni242* was Becca, how much Alia, and how much some combination of Becca and Alia, some fantasy girl. But the thing was, he didn't *need* that fantasy girl, because Alia, the real Alia, was here with him, and even if she wasn't going to tell him she wanted his cock down her throat or his tongue all over her, there were still a million things he wanted to do to her, right here, right now, and so it would probably be a good idea to get started.

16

He was kissing her again. And he was hard already, and as if she hadn't just come, ridiculously intensely, *twice,* she was turning toward him and trying to press herself against him. And it was getting more and more difficult to convince herself that this was something that had happened accidentally, something that wouldn't happen again, something she could call it quits on anytime, before more harm was done.

Because she wanted to do it again. As many times as he wanted her to, she would be ready to give him what he needed. It was a little bit of a problem, actually.

A little bit of a Nate addiction.

And Jake had been worried about *his* bad judgment.

Oh, man.

It was probably not even possible to catalog the number of ways having sex with him had been a bad idea.

Add to all the others, the fact that the past refused to stay put. That he was still thinking about her original betrayal, still trying to sort out how much she'd interfered with his relationship with Becca. And the messages had been a low moment. Not the lowest, maybe, but damn low.

She'd had a terrible evening that night. For once, her date—an online match—was the same age he claimed, the same weight he'd appeared in his photo, and had the same job he'd mentioned in his profile. He was even attractive, attractive enough that she'd felt a flare of optimism when he'd met her in the lobby of the restaurant. But it turned out he was angry and bitter, raging against politicians and various ethnic groups and working moms—pretty much no one was immune. Finally, she'd extricated herself, begged off dessert—which told you something about the degree of her desperation—and fought off his unwanted good-night advance.

By then she'd been quite drunk. She almost never drank much, but it had been her only defense against his awfulness. She had let herself into the apartment that she and Becca were sharing—it was before Becca had moved out and found her own place—and, in the dark and quiet, began to cry.

Not just about the awful date. Also about how in just a few days, when his flight finally came through, Nate was going to come home and Becca was going to tell him the truth and it was going to be over. For good.

About missed chances and bad choices, good intentions sliding down the ravine to hell, and the loneliness of knowing that you'd fallen in love with someone who didn't know who you were.

Across the room, the desktop computer, which they shared, pinged. Alia crossed the room and wiggled the mouse.

There was an instant message window up on the screen.

NateRiordan199: Still waiting. They say probably tomorrow. I'm dying of boredom. Please tell me you're awake.

She could feel his disquiet. The long hours, the adrenaline he could never quite burn off. How itchy it must make him. How bored, and how lonely.

I still know you, she thought. *Even if you don't know me.*

It was, oddly enough, a small comfort. The fact that she could feel him, across all this distance. Across her own mistakes and regrets.

She knew she was woozy. She knew her judgment was impaired by both drink and fatigue—it had been a hell of a week at work.

What she didn't count on was her own boredom and loneliness. Matching his.

MenInUni242: What are you doing to kill time?

There wasn't really any harm to *chatting*, right? All the damage had been done.

NateRiordan199: Playing cards. Reading magazines. Playing with my RainGlobe. Wishing I had more Cow Chip cookies. Reading the same books again. I've read Gone Girl *three times.*

MenInUni242: Ouch.

NateRiordan199: And, you know, jerking off. Number one boredom killer.

"Oh!" said Alia, aloud. She'd felt it in the pit of her stomach. No. Truth. Her whole body had flared warm, a sweet, melting burn.

He was not just bored, but desperate, then. A guy alone in a dry and mountainous country, surrounded by men who were buddies but not friends, bored out of his mind, needing contact. Needing—escape. Release.

She tried, unsuccessfully, not to think of his hand on his cock, of the skin taut—

It was sad. And oddly sweet. And hot. And Alia felt all of that, and more, moving underneath her skin, in her chest and belly, *lower.*

Now would be a good time to walk away. But Alia's head was full of the words. The words Nate needed. Soft words, slippery words, sticky words. Achy words. Broken, reaching, yearning, sweet, raw words.

Her head hurt. Her chest hurt.

MenInUni242: Need any help with that?

NateRiordan199: I wouldn't refuse that offer.

MenInUni242: How can I be of assistance?

NateRiordan199: Pretend I'm there. Tell me what you want.

Oh.

Ohhhh.

She'd never been particularly good at that, but she was dying to now. Dying. All achy through and through, and worst of all in her fingertips because of how much she wanted to tell him. Tell him everything.

Maybe it was easier because it was dark. Because she was alone. Because the bad week and the bad night had reduced her resistance to zero. Because she wasn't herself.

MenInUni242: I want your tongue all over me.

The room was dark, the glow of the computer screen the only light. She felt floaty and unreal, unmoored.

NateRiordan199: What else? What else do you want?

MenInUni242: I want you to pin me down.

A long silence, her imagination more vivid than the blue glow of the screen. His weight on her, his hands on her wrists, his hips pressing hers down, as real as the smooth keys under her fingertips. More real.

NateRiordan199: More.

MenInUni242: I want your cock in my mouth. As much as I can hold.

NateRiordan199: Fuck thats hot.

He was a careful typist, usually. Everything well punctuated, correctly spelled, grammatically assembled. So she noticed the omitted apostrophe.

MenInUni242: Having trouble typing?

NateRiordan199: 1 hand

MenInUni242: Where's the other hand?

NateRiordan199: Whr d u thk?

She didn't touch herself. Not yet. The words were intense enough, the ragged syntax. Her breath ragged, too, rapid and uneven in the quiet room. The anticipation, like something expanding in her chest.

And then there was another sound. Barely louder than her breathing, but real. The sound of a bed frame creaking softly as someone turned over and resettled in the other room.

Becca.

Alia had forgotten her completely. She'd been in a trance, the rest of the world fallen away. She'd forgotten *herself,* who she was—and wasn't.

Oh, God, what had she done?

Whatever it was, she had to undo it as best and as quickly as humanly possible.

MenInUni242: I have to go.

NateRiordan199: What!?

Punctuation. He was using both hands again.

MenInUni242: I'm so sorry. More later—

Except, of course, there wouldn't be. Not later, not ever.

"Alia?" Becca came blinking out of the bedroom. "How was your date?"

The full impact of what she'd done was bearing down on her. Lied, pretended, deceived, and—worst—betrayed.

"Oh, *God,* Becca—"

Becca's face was creased with sleep and confusion. "Really bad date?"

And then the tears spilled down Alia's face, the words from her mouth—*I've done something terrible . . . I've made things so much more complicated. I've made your breakup harder . . . I've betrayed you.*

Three days later, Nate's flight landed.

A day after that, Becca came home to the apartment after their date and sank onto the couch beside her sister.

"I think you were right," Becca said heavily. "This isn't the kind of story with a happily-ever-after." And then: "It was the care package that made him angriest. He kept wanting to know why I'd let you put it together, and I couldn't—I just couldn't tell him it was because I didn't care enough."

It meant a ton to me to feel like someone out there gets *me.*

I'm still out here, she wanted to call to him.

But she'd done enough damage.

17

A nd now he knew she'd written those messages.

It probably wouldn't be long until he would put two and two together and realize the rest of the truth. That she'd written those messages because she'd felt them, felt every last word. Because she'd wanted him. Because she'd *loved* him. Maybe from the beginning. Certainly from that letter, the one right before the care package, where he'd told her in such beautiful, intricate detail what he loved in the world.

So similar to what she loved in the world.

She didn't want him to know. She never wanted him to know. Because this had to be temporary, and it would make the inevitable end so much more humiliating if Nate knew how she felt. How long and how deeply she'd felt it.

She pulled away. Looked into his eyes, hoping to see his trepidation peering back at her. But all she saw was that *look.* The one he'd given her when she'd gotten naked for him, the one that said he was thinking about how to glory in the treasure that he'd uncovered. His eyes were hot and dark and his mouth was wet from their kiss and she wanted to lick his lower lip.

But she made herself say what needed to be said.

"You should probably go."

He shook his head. "I know you're a little wigged out by this—"

"Not wigged out. But—realizing we have a problem."

"We don't," he said sternly. "We do *not* have a problem. We have chemistry. We have amazing sex. We don't have a problem."

Chemistry. Amazing sex. Very flattering, but not what she'd most wanted him to say.

"But we will have a problem if you stay and someone sees you leaving in the morning."

"Will we? Will we really?"

Not the most terrible problem on earth, but it was so much easier to make this all about Jake and the job than to dig into the mess of the past. *I've loved you for so long. From the beginning. I was the one who fell for you. That night, those messages—I wanted to tell you everything about how I felt and what I wanted. This isn't just sex for me, and I know it can't be anything more than that for you—*

And why? So he could give her a pitying look and remind her, again, that he had people to take care of?

Instead, she stuck with the simplest of all the truths she knew. "I promised Jake I wasn't interested in anything with you."

"You apparently lied."

She loved that cocky grin, and it wore down her resistance. Sad, but true.

"I misjudged."

"You lied. Admit it."

He gave her a stern, dark look, and she looked back, something inside her unwinding and melting in the heat of his gaze, and then he was kissing her again, and she was kissing him, too. Like they'd kissed earlier, like there would be no stopping this thing. He was moving his body weight on top of hers, and her breasts tightened and her hips lifted and she pressed her pubic bone against the length of him, and he was reaching for a condom and Oh. My. God. She was swollen from before and so wet and he was bigger than anyone she'd ever been with. He filled her and stretched her and maybe it was how primed she was from the other two orgasms, but she could swear she was going to come again, and it wasn't going to take much.

He was in no hurry this time, though. And that was a good thing. Slow, long, strokes, and because she was so aroused already, she could feel the whole length of each one, all slick and glittery-feeling, setting off nerves that she didn't think had ever fired before, nerves whose other ends were everywhere in her body so it felt like he was touching her breasts, too, her hands, her feet, her belly—*gah*. And then he *was* touching her all over, mouth on her nipples, alternating, smiling at her in between, moving slowly from one to the other, light at first and then firmer and firmer as she arched her back under him and rose to meet him, as his strokes got longer and slicker and sweeter and deeper, as they found new parts of her that swelled and squeezed and clenched and *craved*. Until he was pulling so hard on one nipple that it was one long continuous tug deep into her core, until it felt like her nipple *was* her clit and she was coming, saying his name, loudly enough that if someone had been passing in the hallway they would have heard her.

But he didn't stop then. He kept thrusting in, drawing out, her hand on his ass now so she could feel the bunch of muscle. The ins and outs blended together. The boundaries blurred—the ones between her mouth and his, between his breath and hers, between the heat of him inside her and the heat of her body, and finally between his cries and hers.

Several minutes later he raised his head and said, "Wow."

She had lost the power of speech. Or even sound.

"Two more," he said proudly. "Now. You were saying?"

She watched him get up and dispose of the condom. He came back and lay down and wrapped her up. She liked that he did that. That he cuddled. He didn't seem, on the surface, like he'd be a cuddler, although she supposed she had already known about him that he liked to be touched. That he liked it a lot.

She sighed. "I have to tell Jake. Before he finds out from someone else. Before someone sees us together or sees you leaving here."

"Why do you have to tell him? I'm not your client. It's not his business who you sleep with."

"I wish it were that simple. But for one thing, like I said, I told him this wasn't going to happen. So I think I owe it to him, at least, not to be lying to him. Purposely or not. And the truth is, even though you're not my client, you were, and it's not really the image that I think Jake wants R-and-R to project. It's a little too much the whole massage-with-a-happy-ending thing."

"What do you think he'll say?"

"I think—" Her heart clenched at the thought. "I think

there's at least a good possibility he'll tell me he can't seriously consider giving me the job."

Nate looked gratifyingly appalled at that. "Do you really think that?"

"He's a pretty upright guy. And he really loves this place. I could see him wanting to avoid even the appearance of wrongdoing."

"God, I hope not. I'll feel like shit if that happens."

"I'll make the best argument I can that he should still take me on." She sighed. She should be angrier at herself. Angrier at both of them. But she couldn't quite bring herself to regret what had passed between them. Not while she could still feel the imprint of his touch all over her body. Inside. "And—" She hesitated, knowing she was laying down a gauntlet of sorts. "I'll tell him that I'll leave R-and-R until you're gone."

"Wait. What do you mean you'll leave?"

"So there's less chance of someone seeing us together, even just talking or flirting. Less chance that someone will make too much of something."

"Do you mean like leave leave? Like, we won't . . . have sex again?"

Unless he was faking it, he *really* didn't like that possibility. And, okay, that made hope brim in her chest, which she was going to have to crush flat before he did it for her.

"What were you expecting? You've got J.J.'s family. I've got my work. And what is this, anyway? I mean, really? It's good sex."

"Great sex," he corrected. "Make that phenomenal sex."

That made her smile. "Phenomenal sex," she admitted, loving the grin he gave her in return. "But you're not in a place for anything serious, and neither am I. So doesn't it make sense for us to call it what it is, get everything out in the open with Jake, and quit before someone gets hurt?"

"Sure, yeah—I guess—but right away? Do we have to tell him immediately?" There was a little-boy innocence about the question, like he was negotiating for one more cookie at dessert. And the conjunction of that and the not-so-little-boy way he was looking at her made her want to agree to what he was proposing. Secrecy. Stolen time. More, more, more of his mouth on her nipples, his hands in her hair, that rhythm he knew *exactly* how to set between her legs.

But it would come back to bite her in the end. Because in the scheme of things that could break her heart, not getting the R&R job wasn't the worst. "I think we should tell him."

"And you think he'll definitely want you to leave."

"I think . . . I think it's the most likely outcome."

He was quiet for a moment, his gaze distant. Then he turned back to her, grinning again, and *damn,* she liked that grin way too much. "Well, let's wait and see what he says. Maybe it won't be as dire as all that."

He reached out and stroked her hair, and she felt it then. The shift that had taken place. The hole that had opened up inside her. The realization that a few hours had changed everything. Sex had changed everything for her, had connected her to him in a way that she wasn't going to be able to easily forget.

The crazy thing about what had passed between her and Nate, both last time and this time, was that she kept breaking her own heart. She couldn't even blame him for it. She kept putting them in these situations where she was bound to feel more than he did.

Tears came to her eyes. She turned away so he couldn't

see them. She knew she should tell him to go. The longer he stayed, the more her heart would break in the end. But she couldn't quite say it. Instead, she let him touch her hair, the side of her face, her lower lip, a glancing brush of his finger that sent sensation soaring through her whole body. And when he kissed her again, she let him, and when he opened his arms to her, she curled into them, and she closed off her mind and opened her heart and let herself have this night with him.

JUST BEFORE DAWN, after a few hours of drugged, postcoital sleep Nate woke with Alia in his arms. He was hard again, and he thought of waking her slowly and sliding into her before she was quite fully aware of him, of what a pleasure it would be to ease her out of drowsiness and into arousal.

She'd still be slick and swollen from the sex earlier, and she'd kiss him sleepily and wrap her arms around his neck. The last time he'd made love to her she'd made these small, soft whimpering noises, and she'd do that again, and those sounds had gotten under his skin so bad it made his chest hurt to think about.

But then after that it would be time for him to go.

He was still hopeful she wouldn't tell Jake. That her courage would fail her—even though he couldn't see it—she was so stalwart about so much.

Or that Jake would dismiss it. *He's not your client. It's not a big deal.*

Something. Something to buy them a little more time. To

buy him a little more time to be in her arms, cradled between her thighs, held in the clutch of her body.

But he knew Jake, too, and he knew her assessment was dead-on. That wasn't a likely outcome. Nate just hadn't—he hadn't seen it all the way through in his mind. He hadn't thought about the fact that once they'd crossed this line, she'd feel compelled to confess. And once she confessed, Jake would have no choice but to do something decisive to protect R&R. And even if that didn't mean taking away the job opportunity from Alia, it almost certainly did mean an end to what was happening right now. To this strange time-out-of-time experience of holing up here with her.

And he didn't like that.

"Li," he whispered.

"Mmmmmm?"

The sound dragged across his skin, got his blood up.

"I have to get going. But shower with me first?"

She was adorable, sleepy. Eyes still slitted, shuffling to the shower, turning on the water while half leaning against the wall.

And she was beautiful under the water. Her skin wasn't the same color all over. It was a dark freckle-dappled gold on her face and her shoulders, a paler color on her neck, legs and arms, where the freckles ran even more riot, and the creamiest white over her breasts and belly.

He washed her first. First her hair, silk in his hands. Then the rest of her, smoothing his hands over her skin, the thin layer of soap letting them skate, the slipperiness jacking up sensation so it was like his fingertips were a direct conduit to his cock. He touched her everywhere, lingering when she closed her eyes and opened her mouth and breathed so deep it was almost a moan. Then he slid his body against hers, her smooth thighs, the satin perfection of her breasts, handfuls of soap-slick ass in his grip, hoping briefly he wasn't hurting her and then not caring as he hauled her against him.

So. Tempting. To. Just. Slide. In.

Then her hands were on him. Soapy. Startling him with the suddenness, with the glide—yeah, he'd felt it a million times during solo showers, but holy fuck was it different when it was someone else's hand. Her hand. Startling him, most of all, with her sureness. A good grip, a tight grip, as tight as his own fist, and her pace was good, too, a little faster than he would have started himself out, but it was hot, watching her hand move up and down on him, watching the head emerge from her fingers, swollen and shiny. Watching her watch, too.

Fuck.

"You," she said.

For a moment he thought that was all she was going to say, but then she said, quietly, almost musing, "You are the perfect size. I mean, exactly."

Like she'd been thinking about it. And something about that really got to him, so it was like she'd clutched a little tighter and moved a little faster, and he was suddenly having more trouble not giving in completely to her. Just letting go and watching her watch him come all over her hand.

Which would be so hot. And he let himself fantasize a little about it, which made it even harder not to—

He stayed her hand. Slowed her down, a little.

And she said, in that same musing tone, "You're big enough to *feel* big inside me." And *shit,* it wasn't the touch even, it was the words, and the slight slack to her mouth, like she was thinking about putting her lips to him—

"I love the soft-and-hard thing, too. So smooth"—a finger, swirled around the head—"but no give." She squeezed to demonstrate, and said, "I want it—I want *you* in me again."

I want—

That was what he'd wanted. Just that. Those words in her mouth.

He reached for the condom he'd set on the side of the tub. Pushed her hands away—not gently. She made a noise of protest, but he kissed her, turned her around. From behind her waist was barely wider than a single hand span, while her hips were twice that, her ass the same creamy white as her belly and breasts. He pushed her to the wall, spread her open, entered her, filled her, thrust, thrust again—

"Yeah. Just like that."

Her voice, against the tile, the words a gasp of pleasure as he reached around and cupped her and she ground against his hand, ground down on his cock, her hands sliding down the tile where she couldn't get purchase, until they both had to lean their hot faces and bodies against the cold tile, panting, the water still running, the sound mingling in symphony with their jagged breath.

18

She could feel herself slowing down as she approached the office, her dread manifesting itself.

She knew this was the right thing to do. She and Nate had talked about it.

Her body felt loose and free. Her mind felt—empty. And even though he'd made her come *six times,* every time she let her mind wander back, she felt cavernous with longing for more.

She could lie to herself, but she'd know. What had happened between her and Nate was going to happen until something stopped them—the most likely thing being getting caught. And she didn't want Jake to hear about it from someone else.

Sometime last night, sometime between the first time she came and the sixth, she'd realized that she didn't care anymore about the job. Or, correction: She still cared, but she recognized that it had been sacrificed on the altar of her attraction to Nate. And she was okay with that.

But she wasn't okay with losing Jake's friendship, so this was what had to be done.

In the meantime, Nate had gone down to southern Oregon for a couple of days to gear up for the upcoming weekend with Braden, now only a couple of weeks off. They were going to inventory all their combined camping equipment and go shopping for anything else they needed.

I'll be back late Wednesday, he'd said.

She wondered if he'd been thinking what she was. About whether they'd be able to steal more time together or whether it was already over.

Neither of them had asked the question aloud.

"Is Jake in?"

Sibby looked up from the computer.

"No, hon. Didn't you get his message?"

She shook her head.

"He said he left you a couple voicemails. His mom was in a car accident last night."

Alia's heart contracted, and her face must have blanched, because Sibby said, "She's okay. She's okay. But he won't be in for a couple days."

"Do you think—can I call him? Or should I not bother him?"

"Why don't you see what his messages say?"

"Can we get her some flowers? Or a basket? Something?"

"On it," said Sibby with a smile.

"Can I—" She reached into her purse, snagged two twenties, and handed them to Sibby. Things were hard for Sibby, Alia knew—one son, a bit of a deadbeat, still living at home, and this income hardly enough for one, let alone two.

"No, hon." Sibby tried to hand them back.

"Please. If you get other donations and it's too much, you can give me some back."

Sibby hesitated again, but then her face softened into gratitude and she slipped the money into her pocket. "Thank you, hon."

"Let me know. If there's anything I can do. If you want me to place the order—"

"I got it, love."

Her phone began buzzing persistently. A call.

She pulled it out. It was Jake.

"Oh, Jake."

"Hi, Li." His voice was strained.

"I'm so sorry I didn't call back—Sibby told me—I didn't get the messages—"

They'd probably gotten tangled up in all the texting, flown right by her attention during a moment of bunched-up phone buzzing. Her guilt spiked.

"No worries. I just wanted to make sure you knew I hadn't abandoned you. They think she's going to be fine, but she has whiplash and a fractured rib and they're still keeping a close eye for internal injuries and concussion. She can't remember much, and she's really shaken up. I need to stay. I'm going to stay a couple days, probably. Can you hold down the fort?"

"Of course."

"Have Sibby transfer whichever of my appointments to you she can. Have her postpone the others for a few days. I'm hoping to be away less than a week."

"Don't worry about anything. Just take care of your mom. And take care of yourself."

"You're my hero."

Oh, but I'm so not, she thought. "Jake?"

She was torn. Not wanting to make his life more complicated, not wanting to be selfish, but also not wanting to use his mom's situation as an excuse for dishonesty.

"Wait, hang on—"

Someone was talking to him, a doctor or a nurse, and held the phone a polite distance from her own ear so it didn't feel like she was eavesdropping on him, and—God, he didn't need her little piece of drama right now. *His mom.*

He came back to the phone. "What were you going to say?"

"I—" *I can't tell him right now. The last thing he needs is to be worrying about that while he's trying to help his mom.*

"And don't worry about Nate," Jake said. "He's not on my schedule, but if he needs something in a pinch, text me and I'll come back—I'm only forty-five minutes away."

"He'll be fine. We'll be fine. Don't give us another thought."

"I'm so grateful you're there."

She felt another sharp pang of guilt. And loss. Because he would have been such a good boss. It would have been such a good job.

She hung up the phone and sat on the steps outside the office. Until she realized her dominant feeling was no longer guilt, but relief. As much as she hadn't told Jake the truth for his own sake, she hadn't told him for *her* sake. Because his absence offered her a few more days, a few more days before the moment of reckoning.

A few more days with Nate.

She wanted them, more than she'd ever wanted anything in her life.

ALIA: *Jake's not here. His mom was in a car accident; he'll be out a few days.*

Nate: *Oh, no! She okay?*

Alia: *I think she's fine, just shaken up.*

Nate: *Glad to hear it. Geez. Makes you think, right?*

Alia: *I know.*

She set the phone down and logged in to the patient-records app. Griff was up next. He'd seemed to make a cosmic leap forward in progress since Nate's arrival, further convincing her that one of the foremost healing properties of this place was the way it let veterans be around other guys who'd seen the worst and lived to tell.

Nate: *So you didn't tell him about us?*

She liked it. That *us.* Too much.

Alia: *No.*

Nate: *Does that mean—a little bonus time?*

Bonus time, huh? Like the overtime in a video game when you were pretty much already dead. And even though she knew he'd used those words without thinking, hadn't meant to turn what had passed between them into a transaction, to be enjoyed, prolonged, but ultimately finished, her stomach hurt anyway.

Nate: *Can I see you when I get back Wednesday night?*

Oh, foolish, hopeful heart. *He just wants to get laid again.*

But what if he doesn't want just that? What if he's open to the possibility of more?

She hated how it felt like birds taking off in her chest, thinking about it.

She had missed so many opportunities last night to ask him. If the sex had changed things for him, too, if there could be more for them than "bonus time." And she'd missed the biggest chance of all this morning, when he had stood inside her closed door and kissed her, so tenderly and lingeringly, goodbye. He'd withdrawn his hands from hers with as much reluctance as she'd felt, and he'd looked back at her once before he'd closed the door, and been gone.

She was afraid if she brought the questions out into the open, he'd point out the obvious. That it was one night. That it was too soon, too fast, to draw conclusions or change plans.

It wasn't just that night, she argued with him, silently. *I've known since way back.*

She known. But he hadn't. He'd been in love with a person who looked like Becca and wrote like Alia, and—well, that wasn't her.

Nate: *Can't stop thinking about it. The look on your face when you come.*

Oh, God.

Alia: *I can't, either.*

She needed to sort this all out. To make some sense out of it. And then maybe once she did that, she would know how to talk to him. What to ask him for.

As if the depth of Alia's confusion had conjured her, Becca's photo flashed across Alia's screen and the phone began to ring.

She thought about not answering it, because her thoughts were such a jumble. Because if there was a person on earth to whom she might suddenly blurt out the mess of her thoughts and feelings, it was Becca—and Alia wasn't ready for that.

But she had never not taken a call of Becca's when it had come in, and she wasn't going to start now.

Alia: *Phone call. More in a bit.*

"Hey, big sister." Becca's voice was a balm.

"Hey, little sister."

"I'm so glad you're there." Becca's voice caught. Tears.

Everything shifted suddenly, the way it always did when her baby sister was in trouble. "Are you okay?"

"No. No." Another catch, this one almost a sob. "I make a mess of everything."

"No! You don't. Hon, absolutely not."

It felt good to comfort her sister. The one time things had been reversed, on that terrible night when Alia had sent Nate the instant messages, it had felt all wrong. She'd hated that night, the way she'd broken down, the tears and sobs, Becca patting her head and offering awkward comfort. It had made her understand why parents don't cry, the wrongness of having your child offer you solace. It felt like weakness and, worse, she knew she didn't deserve the sympathy, didn't deserve the generosity of Becca's total forgiveness. Becca kept saying all the right things, *You knew I wasn't into him anymore. I knew you liked him. It was bound to happen, the way you felt, keeping that inside all that time, all those letters that weren't for you.* And *It's going to be okay, I promise.* And *Please stop beating yourself up.*

That, of course, had been beyond impossible.

Becca's sob recalled her to the present.

"Oh, hon. Tell me what happened."

"I don't know. I don't know. I—I freaked out is what

happened. And now it's been three days, nothing. That can't be a good sign, can it?"

"It was the third date?"

"Fourth."

"Can you give me any details? Not the gory ones—" Alia amended quickly.

She'd pulled a shaky laugh from Becca, and she felt the relief that accompanied having a concrete problem to solve. A sister to soothe, someone to heal, something easier to fix than her own romantic difficulties. All her irritation with her sister vanished, and she perched on the table so she could concentrate on her sister's story.

"He's like—he's this great guy. Super-smart, started his own computer company, now he's like a bajillionaire with a staff and going to get bought out by Google or Amazon or whoever any minute. But totally down-to-earth. So nice. And so romantic with me—all the wining and dining, and telling me he really liked me, making me believe it, and telling me he was starting to care for me."

"And then?"

"And then—we went back to his place, and oh, God, it was amazing—this guy can seriously—never mind, you said no gory details, but you know—"

"Did you guys actually—?"

"No. I'm still an everything-but virgin," Becca said, with a note of bitterness. "Not that I'm complaining, like I said, but — Anyway, afterward, we're on the couch, and it's getting late, the heat shut off, and he gets up to go get a blanket for us—"

"Aw," Alia said.

"I know, right? And I start wandering around, looking at his books, and I totally freak out. Looking at book after book after book I've never read and I'll probably never read, and he comes back and I freeze up. Totally freeze. So I ran away."

"Because of his books?"

"Because—because he said—being able to talk to someone smart and thoughtful and educated is really important to him—"

Becca's voice broke, a sob for real this time.

"He said that when? Last night? When?"

"As we were walking back to his place."

"Before he asked you up? Before he kissed you? Before whatever?"

"Yes."

"So he meant *you,* Becca. He was telling you he thought you *were* smart and thoughtful and educated. Easy to talk to. Because you *are.*"

Someday she'd say it and Becca would believe her. She knew it. But in the meantime she'd tell her as many times as she needed to hear it.

"And since then—nothing." Becca's voice was a whisper.

"You've left messages, texts, all that?"

"Yes. But—I ran out on him without an explanation. He has a right to be angry."

"Yeah, that's not the perfect scenario, sure, but you can still talk about it. What did you say in your messages and texts? Did you apologize? Did you tell him *why*?"

"I—I apologized, but I didn't tell him why."

"You need to tell him why. You need to talk about it."

Becca was silent. She'd never liked to talk about it. Not about her learning disabilities or the self-esteem issues they'd caused.

"If he's a good guy, you can make yourself vulnerable to

him. That's really the only way things are going to work out anyway, right? He needs to know who you are, what you're afraid of, and what you want."

Ah, she was *such* a hypocrite.

It was time. Time for her to tell Nate how she felt, and then they could have The Talk. And she'd see. If maybe there was more wiggle room than she'd thought.

She felt like laughing out loud. And bursting into tears.

Griff poked his head into Alia's office. "You ready for me?"

She nodded, got up from the table, and indicated that he should lie down. "Hey—my patient just walked in."

"I'll let you go. But do you really think it'll work? Telling him?"

Did she? She wasn't sure. She wanted to spout all the right words—*Honesty is the best policy* and *To thine own self* and all that—but did she believe them? Did she believe that all it would take to heal a rift was a bridge of words?

"I think it's worth a try, baby. And let me know how it goes, okay?"

Her sister drew a deep breath. "Okay. Love you. Don't know what I'd do without you."

It wasn't until Alia hung up the phone that she realized she'd never told Becca any of her own story.

Her phone buzzed again.

"Do you mind if I tie up this one loose end?" she asked Griff.

"Take your time." He had his hands behind his head and his legs crossed, the picture of relaxation, even though she knew inside he was as knotted up as any of them.

Nate: *You never answered me. Can I see you tomorrow night?*

Alia: *My room.*

Then, feeling panicky, *Be discreet. I don't want Jake hearing from someone other than me.*

Nate: *Will do.*

A brief silence.

Nate: *In the meantime, will you do something for me?*

She felt what was coming. In the fluttering in her belly and the anticipatory clenching between her legs.

Nate: *Every time you're alone, touch yourself.*

19

They'd started Tuesday morning, gray and heavy with fog, in Braden's granddad's hardware store. The hardware store that had, once, been J.J.'s legacy. That was now his own, and Braden's.

Braden and Jim led him around the store to show him all the new merchandise that had come in since his last visit, and how it improved a hundredfold on what they'd had before. A waffle maker where you could swap out the grids to make panini. A step stool that was stronger than the old one but also folded smaller. A different brand of LED lightbulb that lasted longer.

Nate had summoned up as much enthusiasm as he could, admiring and handling everything he was shown, but he knew he didn't feel what they felt. He didn't nourish the same love for the wall devoted to every head size and thread count of screw you could ever want.

Every screw you could ever want . . . heh. Heh-heh.

His mind went off on a little romp, remembering two

nights ago in ridiculous detail, until he dragged it back to the present.

He didn't want to use too much energy wanting what he might be able to have at most a few more times.

He felt like shit, not only because he was feigning enthusiasm for Jim and Braden's beloved stuff, but also because being here, in the store, had made him start to ask the tougher questions.

Is this really what I want to be doing?

He reminded himself that this wasn't about what he wanted to be doing. J.J. didn't want to be six feet under, a flag and a bronze star and a purple heart sleeping on his bed instead of him. Braden didn't want to be fatherless, more or less an orphan. Jim and Suzy didn't want to have lost their only child, to be in possession of an heirless hardware store.

Life was about doing what had to be done, not about kicking back and getting laid as often as you pleased.

He pushed her, and the memories of the other night, from his mind.

They headed to the camping store next. Braden went nuts in there, too. Funny, he was such an acquisitive little squirrel. That was another thing he'd gotten from his father. J.J.'s pack had been a magpie's nest of pointless junk, weighing him down.

Braden wanted it all. Waterproof notebook. Water purification system that let you suck the stuff straight out of the ground and through a filter. Pocket-sized solar spark lighter. Full-body bug gear.

"You can write in the rain with this pen!" Braden, dark-haired, freckled, and unusually mature and serious for ten, jumped up and down with excitement.

For a kid who had to be in a lot of psychic pain, Braden was in good shape. Nate figured it was because he had such a strong bond with his grandparents, who had taken care of him for the last four years. For his whole life, really, since J.J. had been seventeen when Braden was born, and had spent most of the last ten years overseas.

"Okay. We'll need that," Nate said, straight-faced, and threw the waterproof notebook into the mesh shopping basket for good measure.

"Do we need a kayak?"

"I can borrow kayaks, life vests, paddles, floats, and pumps from R-and-R."

Jake had offered, which had taken a big load off, planning-wise. Nate knew he could find some place to rent them near here, but it would have been expensive.

He had some camping supplies of his own, and Jim and Suzy had some. Plus, they were going for only two nights, so there were just a few things he had to fill in. Iodine tablets, camping MREs—or whatever the civilian term for those vile meals-in-a-pouch was—cookstove gas, groceries.

He still wasn't a hundred percent sure that he could do the trip without pain, but the last couple days had made him more optimistic. He'd kept up with the stretching and strengthening, and he could feel the new flexibility and power in his neck, back, and shoulders. When the pain came, he did all the stuff Alia had showed him. Relaxed his body, corralled his focus, *accepted*. It didn't seem so stupid anymore. A few times now, tricks he'd learned from her had chased the pain back to its source, and he was a believer. Yeah, it still hurt. A lot sometimes. But the pain didn't make him panic, which meant he wasn't tensing up and making it worse. He wasn't escalating it.

Alia had given him a ton of confidence in his own abilities, and some good tools, too. Maybe he'd have some bad moments, but he'd get through them. He knew that.

He checked his phone. For the ten-thousandth time since Saturday. Not that he was expecting minute-by-minute updates, but he'd thought maybe—

He'd hoped, maybe, she'd do what he'd asked.

Every time you're alone, touch yourself.

It had been total whim. Him prodding a little, to see what would come of it.

But there'd been two days of silence.

He sighed.

"Look at all the different ways you can purify water!"

He was a big fan of iodine, personally—lightweight, effective. The only downside was the taste. The vitamin C afterpills would cut through the unbearable iodine flavor, but there was a lingering not-quite-right-ness to treated water. It tasted—oddly enough—dry.

"This is going to taste weird," he warned Braden, but Braden shrugged.

Damn, he could see so much J.J. in him. In that shrug. In the general gameness that the shrug connoted. In the slightly narrowed, considering dark eyes.

He took a package of iodine pills from the display, grabbed one of the small canisters of cookstove gas for his portable stove as they passed them, and led Braden to the camping meals display.

"Okay. What doesn't look like it will taste like dirt?"

"I like spaghetti with meat sauce."

"It won't taste like your grandma's. But when you're camping you probably also won't care. I remember one of the first times I camped I ate this crappy powdered pesto and it was seriously the best food I've ever eaten."

Braden picked out a bunch more of the pouches, and they went to ring up.

"Where you headed?" the cashier asked. He was probably twenty-two, with the soft look of a guy who talked more about camping than he did it.

"Lower Owyhee, kayaking."

"That's a trek."

"I kayaked there as a kid and always wanted to do it again."

"Well, if you want something closer to home—you ever tried Fearsome Lake?"

"Fearsome? Let's go there!" That was the J.J. in Braden again, and for a moment Nate was so slammed with sadness, he couldn't talk. Couldn't even make himself slide the credit card out of his wallet.

Then he collected himself.

"Maybe next time."

He didn't have to love the hardware store. He just had to put one foot in front of the other, for Braden.

THEY WERE UNLOADING everything from the car, getting ready to carry it into Jim and Suzy's house, when his phone buzzed.

He wrenched it out of his pocket so fast he scraped a knuckle.

Alia: *I'm alone. In the office. Any specific instructions?*

Well, hello, *Alia. Game on.* His heart started to pound. He'd given up hope that she'd take his request seriously.

He started to reply.

Hell, yeah—

"Who are you texting?" Braden demanded to know.

He stuffed the phone back in his pocket. "A friend."

The fog had lifted and it was an Oregon summer-blue sky, clear and brilliant. Suzy came to the door, a bright-eyed heron of a woman. "I've got grilled cheese and tomato soup for dinner, boys. Jim is still at the store. He won't be back for a while. Dinner in ten?"

"Sounds good. Hey—you mind if I run out for one more quick errand? And leave Braden with you for a few?"

"Sure! See you soon."

He got back in the car and drove. Drove any old place, till the neighborhood gave way to a dirt road where he could park his car and yank the phone out of his pocket.

Nate: *Okay. Just me now for a few minutes. Where've you been?*

Alia: *You wouldn't believe how busy, doing my patients and Jake's. And then falling into bed and sleeping like the dead.*

Probably sleeping off their all-nighter, he thought, with the first grin he'd managed in a while.

Alia: *But I'm not busy now. You know what they say about idle hands . . .*

Oh, yeah, he did.

He had to think about it for a minute, and double whoa, because there were so many things he could think of, a parade of dirty, dirtier, downright filthy. There were so many parts of her body, soft, smooth, supple, lithe, that he wanted his own hands on, that he could get off imagining *her* hands on.

He'd start her off easy and escalate. *Lick your lips. Slowly. Like you're doing it to turn me on.*

Alia: *Now what?*

No. He wanted more than that.

Nate: *Tell me how it felt.*

Alia: *I pretended you were kissing me.*

Okay. Okay. Better. But still, he wanted more.

Nate: *No. How it felt.*

He didn't really expect a reply. Well, his brain didn't expect a reply. His body was already revving up for one. Cock easing toward fullness. He wondered if it felt the same to her when her body got ready for him. A down-deep tug, a surge of something almost like raw power, and a sense almost like expansion, a sudden hollowing.

Alia: *Like you were licking me. Soft and warm and wet . . .*

Ohhh. Wow, wow, wow. Speaking of a surge of power. If he could get her to play this game with him, if he could draw her out—

The echo caught him. *I want your tongue all over me.*

Forget that. Forget *MenInUni242*. He had *Alia* on the other end of the SMS connection, talking dirty.

Nate: *You know what makes me hot?*

Alia: *What?*

Nate: *When you want it. When I know you want it. Like yesterday, when you were on top of me and I could feel you needing to move.*

There. No more pretending *that* hadn't happened.

Nate: *When I made you come and watched your face.*

The flush, her eyes, her open mouth, the kiss—her so soft with it that her mouth had melted under the thrust of his tongue, and he'd known exactly what it was going to be like to fuck her.

Nate: *Or in the shower. Telling me what you like about my cock.*

Alia: *So many things. Tough to list them all.*

Nate: *You could try.*

Alia: *Did I mention how I love the ridge along the length? And how big the head is?*

He reached for the button of his jeans, then abruptly remembered. *Oh, Jesus, dinner.*

Nate: *Was about to do some serious damage to myself, then realized I'm late to dinner. More soon?*

Alia: *I could finish the list. And tell you some other things I've been thinking.*

Nate: *Stop. Have to have family dinner.*

He set the phone facedown on the passenger seat. It took him quite a few minutes before he was in any condition to drive back to the house.

Ten minutes later, he, Suzy, and Braden were sitting down together when his phone buzzed again.

He would not look at his phone at the table. He would not look at his phone at the table. He would not look at his phone at the table.

A minute later, it buzzed again.

"Do you need to get that?" Suzy asked.

"Nah."

"You sure?"

He took a bite of Suzy's awesome grilled cheese and chased it with a big spoonful of tomato soup, waiting for the craving to die down, but there was no way. There was no way. He wanted—*needed*—to know what she'd written.

"I just—" He shot an apologetic glance at Suzy and Braden, and caught Suzy's eyes narrowing slightly.

Alia: *Do you know what I want to do right now?*

"I'm sorry—let me just quickly—" he told Suzy and Braden.

Nate: *Give me an hour and I'll give you my undivided attention.*

"I thought you said there was no one special."

He was so startled he almost dropped the phone into the tomato soup.

Suzy's arms were crossed, a smirk on her face.

"He said it was a friend," Braden supplied.

Suzy shook her head. "With the number of times Nate's checked that phone in the last two days? And that goofy smile on his face? Uh-uh. I don't think so."

He tried to wipe off whatever expression had given him away, but it was hopeless. He could feel it. His mouth kept wanting to curve into a smile.

"You should bring her to meet us."

She was putting on the bravest possible face, she was smiling at him, her warmest, best smile, but he knew what it was costing her. He knew she was thinking of J.J. and how he wouldn't be bringing anyone home to meet them, and he tried to picture it, tried to picture bringing Alia here, introducing her to Jim and Suzy and Braden, but he just—couldn't. He couldn't see it, as if Alia and the quiet, hidden intimacy of what they'd shared were something in one life and these guys, J.J.'s people, were a whole other life, and the two weren't supposed to mix.

And why should they? Alia had said herself, this was almost over. Why make this more complicated than it had to be?

"It's nothing serious," he said.

Suzy watched his face for a long time, until he had to look away.

20

They'd been going back and forth for hours. After work, as she'd straightened her office and gotten things together for another monumental day tomorrow. After he'd told her to give him an hour, he'd texted again, wanting her to put her finger in her mouth. *Lick it. Really lightly. Like you're teasing.*

She'd been shocked by how good it had felt. The touch of tongue to finger, and the touch of finger to tongue. A feedback loop. She'd gotten so distracted she hadn't reported back and he'd texted: *You better be doing it.*

Alia: *Yes. And enjoying.*

Nate: *Suck it.*

She had to admit, it wasn't only the feel of the suction around her finger, or how much it made her mouth crave something else. It was the pure dirtiness and rawness of the command. It was being commanded. It was the black-and-whiteness of seeing it on her phone screen. The thought that these texts were slipping through gateways, past nerdy guys monitoring communications. The NSA could be getting off on her and Nate right now. That was perversely hot.

Also, *damn.* She'd always been kind of indifferent to blow jobs, but sucking her finger right now? All she could think about was how he'd feel in her mouth—oh, so much bigger than her skinny little finger, and that amazing hard-soft combination.

She'd had to lay off the sexting during dinner for a little bit. Only because it was so rude and Gabi and Melinda kept giving her sidelong knowing glances, and it was hard to be this horny and also eat. And she was feeling self-conscious. About being so wet and swollen and aroused that she could actually smell her own sea-salt scent.

She bet Nate would love that.

As soon as she got back to her room, she told him.

Alia: *I can smell how turned on I am.*

There was a long hiatus before she heard from him, during which she thought maybe she'd gone too far. Thought about softening it or taking it back or—

But the thing was, she'd lost her inhibitions around the time of *Suck it.* And there was really no going back. This was how it had been the day she'd been *MenInUni242.* When she hadn't felt like herself and it had freed her to tell him *exactly* what she needed. What she wanted.

She curled up against the wall, a pillow behind her. She'd changed into PJs.

The urge to touch herself was overwhelming, but she was waiting for his instructions. They came only intermittently. It was massively frustrating. Sometimes a half-hour or more would pass between one and the next, during which she forced herself to ride the waves of desire, which sometimes got so intense they bordered on spasms. Like if she let herself go, she could actually come from wanting him. From reading his words on her screen.

She couldn't just sit and wait for him to text back, so she forced herself to read a little of her book. Then played a few word games on her iPad.

Then she gave in, gave up. If he wasn't going to text, she wasn't going to sit here waiting for him. So every once in a while she absentmindedly ran a hand lightly over herself through her thin pajama pants. Keeping herself at the same full-on state, buzzing with anticipation. She'd give him a little more time, but if she didn't hear from him soon—

Nate: *Um. You just killed like ten million of my brain cells. Also, my hand is in my pants.*

She was so wet.

Alia: *You're ruining another perfectly good pair of panties . . .*

Nate: *You know what got me going? How hard your nipples were that day after swimming. I kept trying not to stare at them through your bathing suit. Are they hard now?*

Alia: *Y*

Nate: *I'm hoping you're abbreviating because you're touching them.*

Alia: *Y*

She was. And oh, *man.* Her whole body tightened around that light touch. She was so wound up she could barely sit still.

Nate: *Tell me.*

Alia: *Have to stop touching to tell.*

Nate: *Ups the anticipation.*

It did. And it slowed her down a little, too, which was probably a good thing.

Alia: *Through my tank top. Feels really really good.*

Nate: *Keep doing that. How long do you think it would take you to make yourself come?*

Alia: *Not very long. Embarrassingly short.*

Nate: *Don't. Don't make yourself come.*

She actually groaned aloud.

Alia: *Are you fucking serious?*

She looked over at the clock. It was almost ten. He'd been ratcheting up the tension, messing with her head, basically engaging in long-distance foreplay, for more than four hours.

Nate: *Yes. Also seriously fucking hard. Also very serious about what I am going to do to you when I get there.*

Alia: *I don't think I can wait till tomorrow night.*

She tried to think about whether there had been a time in her life—at least past the age of seventeen or so—when it had seemed so urgent to get off that she had been unwilling to wait twenty-four hours. Now she wasn't sure she could wait twenty-four minutes.

There was a knock on the door.

He didn't let her talk. He grabbed her and kissed her. And she hadn't been lying. Everything she'd told him—that sea-fragrant sex smell wafting up to him, her nipples knots against his chest even through two layers of fabric. He let her go long enough to yank his T-shirt over his head, and she said, "You're here! You're supposed to be in Oregon."

"I figured if we were in bonus time I'd better make good use of it. Drove straight back after dinner."

Then the tank top was gone, too, and he groaned and dipped his head and worked her nipples, one, then the other.

"Nate, you seriously don't understand, you can't do that, I'm going to come if you keep doing that—"

"And what would be wrong with that?"

"The whole time you were texting? The whole time, all I could think about was how good it was going to feel when you were finally inside me because I am seriously—I am so hot and so wet and so swollen, and you are *cruel*—and I want to come with you filling me up and I think I deserve that, don't you?"

He'd never heard that much sex come out of her mouth; plus, she was grinning at him so evilly, and he *knew,* he seriously, seriously *knew,* but right now was *not* the time for talking about it, right now was the time for kissing the shit out of her, which he did, and pulling her clothes off, which he was doing, and shoving his jeans and briefs down—while trying to keep kissing her, which was a trick—and flailing around like an idiot for a condom.

"Wait." She put a firm hand around him, knelt beside him, and lowered her head.

Ohhhhhh.

This was his secret vice. Well, one of them. The look of a woman's lips stretched around his cock. The bobbing of her head, the feel of her fingers wrapped around the base.

It was a little-discussed problem in the world that a lot of women sucked at giving head. No pun intended.

Alia was not one of them. Alia was born to give head. It kind of felt like she had three tongues in there. And she was sucking, pulling, drawing so hard on him that it was right on the jagged edge of perfect.

He groaned.

She hummed her response.

Whoa, nelly.

And that, right there, was the back of her throat, and she did some kind of neat swallowing thing that was like a strong caress over his head, and he. Was. Not. Going. To. Lose. It. In. Her. Mouth. Not when he knew she was ready and willing, and *talking about it,* and he'd gotten her all worked up and swollen, so she was going to be tight—

He pulled away—in the nick of time—and sucked a few lungfuls of air while yanking out the night table drawer, trying to think about anything except the raging storm she'd whipped up in him.

He fumbled the condom on. There was really no other way to describe it. And she lay back and watched him, eyes amused but also dark and admiring.

God, that look.

She cupped her breasts in her hands and began to toy with her nipples. "This is what I was doing before," she remarked, casual, as if she were informing him that she'd just been to the grocery store for milk and a loaf of bread.

He couldn't tear his eyes away. Her fingertips rolling, pinching, tweaking—he reached, and she backed out of his reach, crawled off the bed, and then they were up and he was chasing her around the room. He caught her near the door and backed her against it and pinned her, then ducked his head and took a nipple in his mouth and teased it until she whimpered. Then the other.

"Don't fuck with me," he said.

Another whimper, this one from the soul. And then she whispered, "What if I like fucking with you?"

He scooped her up and carried her back to the bed. Set her down, pushed her onto her back, climbed over her. Was in her in one long, deep, stroke, her body just as she'd said, so wet, so hot, so *ready* for him that she offered no resistance, just the slide home, and then her tight around him, clinging to him, rocking her hips to meet him thrust for thrust. And for each time he filled her, she made a small, distinct sound, half moan, half victory yell, her cries rising in volume and intensity until it was that, the sound of her taking what she wanted and *owning it* that pushed him over the edge.

"WHAT I DON'T UNDERSTAND," she said, millennia later, "is if you were driving back, how were you texting? Were you driving and sexting?"

He shook his head. "Pulled over a few times."

"Oh, *really*. So, like, side of I-five, hand in your pants?"

They were lying side by side, facing each other, and he was grinning at her.

"Yep. Because you're hot. Because sexting with you is hot. And fun. You're fun, you know that?"

And then his expression changed completely. Got serious, and a little—almost harsh. "So tell me. The instant messages. *MenInUni242.* You-being-Becca? Or you-being-you?"

Ohhh. This.

If she told him the truth, she'd be as good as saying, *That was me getting totally carried away, forgetting that I was supposed to be helping Becca. That was me, totally into you, lusting after my sister's boyfriend, getting lost in what I needed and wanted for a few minutes.*

"I don't see—what difference does it make?"

"It makes a huge difference." He stared at her, long enough that she had to look away. "Okay, let me ask you this. I don't remember everything about that IM exchange, but I do remember a few choice phrases. Such as, 'I want your cock in my mouth. As much as I can hold.'"

Oh. Yup. He held her eyes till she had to turn away, blushing.

"You got my cock in your mouth earlier—was it all you'd hoped for?"

Actually, better. As in bigger, thicker, harder, more velvety against her tongue than her imagination had been able to conjure.

"I think you also said, 'I want you to pin me down.'"

He remembered. He remembered everything she'd said. Because it had mattered to him. She'd mattered to him. She —the woman he now knew to be Alia.

"Nate—"

"I did that just now, too. How did it compare to your fantasy?"

"Can't we drop this?"

"No. Were you pretending to be Becca?"

He speared her with his gaze, and the intensity of the way he'd watched her face during sex had *nothing* on this. "You know I was."

"But were you really? I mean, you were sitting there thinking, *Now what would Becca say?* Because not to be crass, but when Becca and I were making out, that whole side of her didn't really come out, if you know what I mean."

Being reminded that he'd kissed Becca felt like being punched in the stomach.

He rubbed his forehead. "Damn. I'm sorry. That was dickish. Look . . . we never . . . Becca and I never. Partly because . . . because she didn't seem that into it. And I never wanted to drag anyone kicking and screaming. I like a woman who . . . who knows what she wants. I need to know, Li." He looked straight at her. "When you wrote that stuff, who was that?"

She closed her eyes.

I like a woman who knows what she wants.

She did, at least when she was in the same room with him. She'd known exactly what she'd wanted when she'd climbed on top of him last night, exactly what she'd wanted when he'd interrupted the meditation to kiss her. Exactly what she'd wanted every step of the way. And yet putting it into words . . .

"Alia." His voice was very quiet, a low rumble. "You're not very good at saying what *you* want, are you?"

An ache began, to the left of her breastbone. She took a deep breath.

"It was me," she said quietly. "Me being me."

When she opened her eyes, he was still gazing at her. His eyes warm, a slight smile pulling at the corners of his mouth. "I thought so. I hoped so."

He gave her that same wicked look he'd worn when he'd made her come against her will.

"So you meant that other part, too? When you said, 'I want your tongue all over me?'"

21

He didn't wait for her to answer. He lay down next to her and drew her close and kissed her. Well, really, he licked her. Because that's what she'd said she'd wanted, so that's what she'd get. His tongue on her upper lip, following the curve of it, savoring the taste of it. His tongue sliding across hers. His tongue on her lower lip—he had to make himself not use his teeth, because she made him want to dig in and hold on. Then he went on a very delicate exploration of her face. More lips than tongue, really, except at the edge of her jaw and her ears, and then only the tip. Tracing and tasting.

Her skin was unbelievably soft. She thrashed when he drew a line from beneath her earlobe down to her throat. She moaned when his mouth found the pulse at the base of her throat. Her whole body arched under him when he nuzzled her neck.

So good. So gratifying.

The whole point here was to spend an eternity getting to his final destination. To make her spend that whole eternity thinking about where he was going and what he was going to do when he finally got there.

When his pain had been so bad, he'd thought a lot about how much he hated his body. How weak and easily hurt bodies were. He'd seen so many bodies broken, so many lives bled out on rock and sand, and his pain reminded him of all of them.

Right now, he loved his body. He loved his hands (which were holding her immobile under him) and his tongue, which had found the upper curve of her right breast, and his cock, which was pressed against her leg in a way that was supposed to be casual but which utterly failed at casual because it kept throbbing and jumping to get more contact. He loved his body because it wasn't causing him pain but giving him pleasure, but mainly he loved his body because it was giving *her* pleasure.

And her body was so receptive and so honest with him about how much pleasure he was giving it. All those quick indrawn breaths and little sighs, moans and groans and whimpers and squeaks, and those low, dark sounds she made, barely voiced breaths. Her nipples hard and tight, the salt scent of her rising arousal, goosebumps and shivers, a tremor that ran all the way through her. He wanted to thank her for it, for all of it, because no one had ever really given him that much before. That much *yes.*

He circled one nipple, then the other, making sure to linger when she shivered and moaned, when his tongue teased underneath her breast and around the outer curve, when his nose accidentally touched ticklish skin under her arm—he stayed all those places and made sure he drew all the possible pleasure from her. He traveled down the planes and slope of her belly, slowly, so slowly, and dipped into her navel and lingered there, too, because it made her squirm.

"You're *killing* me."

"That's the point."

"Lower."

He laughed wickedly and went on finding all the little spots on her abdomen that were ticklish and sensitive. Meanwhile, his hands moved lower and pinned her thighs, his thumbs so close to her center that he could feel her wetness on her leg.

And then he licked his way right down to the edge of her curls and stopped, to mess with her head. Because it made her all wiggly and pissed off, and that turned him on.

She smelled so good. Dark and secret and clean. He spent a while enjoying that. And enjoying the way she shifted her hips as his breath brushed her curls. He blew deliberately, cooler air across the damp, and she made a sweet little broken sound. He got closer and tried to see how hot he could make his breath, and how cool. How broad and soft he could puff air, how directly he could blow it like an arrow against her clit, which had stiffened enough to peek out.

She was impatient now. She was raising herself up to get closer, tilting and rolling for the sake of the motion itself.

He withdrew his breath and then gave it to her again, to see what she'd do, and she let out a gust of a sigh and tried to push herself into his face, but he pinned her hips hard with his hands and wouldn't let her move. Then he savored the strength in those hips, the way she tried to lever herself back into favor.

"Something you want?" he inquired idly.

"I hate you."

He laughed. "You might hate me," he said. "But I know you love *this*."

With the tip of one finger, he began tracing lines. The top edge of her curls. The junctures where her thighs met her torso, one on each side. And the seam of her sex. But so lightly he was only touching hair, brushing it so she'd feel the tickle of his touch. All the way down, skimming where her curls were damp and parted to reveal her, pink and glistening.

That line, over and over again. This time, skimming her clit with his finger so lightly he could barely feel it himself, but she bucked. And then dipping his finger so he could feel how slick she was. She was so wet that his touch could only just have registered, but there her hips went again, wild for contact.

He parted her painstakingly slowly, letting his thumbs glide over her. Opening outer and inner folds to unveil her. He leaned in and touched the tip of his tongue to her swollen clit. Flicked. Then put the flat of his tongue against her and held still, to see what she'd do.

"Ohhh," she said, and rocked her hips to slide her clit across his tongue. He held still and let her. "Don't move," she commanded.

Yes. Tell me.

He obeyed her for long enough to let her start to feel the tension build, then drew back. She groaned deep in her chest.

He spread her open again and licked her.

Unh.

So wet. So slippery, saliva, lube, one eager surface sliding against another, the glossy satin of her slick against his tongue. He was losing control again—she did this to him. It made him want to pin her and punish her, to constrain and control her so he could get his own control back, but she was moving under his mouth and his hands so frantically that he couldn't keep her still, rising up to get more of him, wiggling against him, and finally the only thing he could do to master her was to draw her clit into his mouth and suckle it until she came, yelling and thrashing.

Whereupon he lifted his face and said, "If I don't get inside you in the next three seconds, I'm going to come all over you," and she said, "I want you to come all over me," and he said, "Oh, God, Li," which got lost in a groan, as he lurched to his knees and came all over her belly, barely aware of her hands joining his to squeeze and stroke the last drops onto the smooth pearl of her skin.

22

"I'm sor—"

"If you apologize, I'm going to kill you," Alia said. "First of all, I asked you to do it. And like you said, I'm not good at asking. Well," she said, reconsidering. Because it seemed that things had changed. Most things. Maybe everything. "I wasn't good at asking before you. And also—it was hot. *I liked it.* It's going in the porn library."

"Well, good," he said. "Because I seem to have very little control when it comes to you." He went to the bathroom and came back with a washcloth and began to clean her up.

"Oh," she said. "That's nice and warm."

Another thing to like about Nate. It had occurred to him to warm up the water to wash her. There were way too many things to like about him, actually. She didn't want to like all those things about him, not when she had so little idea how he felt about her.

And right. She owed him—owed *herself*—a conversation. About what this was. About where this was going. About whether it could go anywhere at all.

A conversation that could have only one outcome that wouldn't leave her heartbroken. Particularly after what had just happened. Not so much what he'd done to her—although, *oh, God,* what he'd done to her! But what he'd said.

You're not very good at saying what you want, are you?

And what she'd said. What she'd admitted to.

It was me. Me being me.

Which was, in effect, her admitting to having loved him all along. So, really, there weren't too many secrets left, were there?

"Nate," she said.

"Yeah?"

She hesitated, because she wasn't sure what she wanted to say. What she needed to ask.

"I don't want to stop. Doing this. Being with you."

Startled, he turned to face her. His expression softening. "Oh," he said.

Just that. *Oh.*

It held so much in it. His surprise, and his pleasure, too. How much he liked that she'd said that—she could see it, right there in his face. And the moment drew out and wound tight around them and she was suspended in it. Joyful and terrified.

"I don't want to stop, either," he said.

He pulled her close. Kissed her, not hard the way he had when he'd come into the room earlier after they'd edged each other up into madness, but so sweetly.

"But I have to."

That had been in the *Oh,* too.

"I'm going to this super-small town where there's nothing.

Nothing for you. And you're staying here. Where there's nothing for me."

"I don't have to stay here. I—we—could go to Seattle—"

There was an edge of desperation in her voice she didn't like. Didn't like at all.

And he was shaking his head.

"I never told you. Why it matters to me. The store, and Braden, and the trip, and Suzy and Jim—those are J.J.'s parents.

"No," she said quietly. "You never told me." And suddenly it seemed an enormous omission. One that she should have noticed. That she should have asked about. That she should have demanded he remedy.

"I want to tell you now. If you want to hear."

Too little. Too late.

But yes. She wanted to hear. She wanted to know. She wanted every last bit of him he would give her, even if it made the heartbreak worse later. Because that was how things were now.

"Tell me," she said, and tried not to think about how they'd used those words in another context earlier.

"When I first got here, I had this conversation with the guys. About promises. The ones you say out loud and the ones you keep to yourself. Like this guy who promised his buddy he'd take all the dangerous missions so the guy could get home to his wife and kids."

He didn't have to tell her how that had turned out. She saw it behind his eyes.

"And I was thinking about how even when you don't say them out loud, some things are promises. Like when a guy leaves his wife to go off to war, there are promises. He's saying, *I'll come home.* She's saying, *I'll be here.*"

He looked into the far-off distance. Farther away than she'd ever seen him look, even in those early days when he'd been in so much pain. That seemed like forever ago already. Just a few weeks and he was a different man. Stronger. Sounder.

He didn't need her anymore, not the way he had.

It made her happy, and it made her very, very sad. Because it had been how much he needed her that had made this all happen. And now that he didn't—

"Anyway, I made a promise. I didn't mean to, but I did."

She could feel dread pooling in her stomach. Because even when he'd told her the story of what had happened to J.J., and she'd known how much guilt he was carrying around, even when she knew that guilt was causing him actual physical pain, she hadn't seen, not clearly, how inextricably tied he still was to the past. Now she could see it. Hear it. In the far-off look. In the word "promise."

"It was a couple weeks before the RPG hit the tower. We were doing guard. Near the end of a four-hour shift, both of us tired as dogs. J.J. didn't—he wasn't the kind of guy who wanted to talk philosophy. More, we'd just be both playing video games, and then he'd want to talk about who was hotter, Megan Fox or Kate Upton."

She didn't ask him who was hotter. He was serious, terribly serious now. Not the guy who'd wanted to play, who'd egged her on. This other man, someone she didn't—

Someone she didn't know.

"All of a sudden, he says, 'It's not what I thought. I

thought I'd feel like I was seeing the world and having adventures, and instead it feels like I'm in a cage.'"

"It's J.J., and I'm still not taking him too seriously, so I gesture at the windows of the guard tower and say, 'We are in a cage.' But he gives me this look, and I shut up. He says, 'I wanted so bad to get away from that store, and now all I want to do is get back there and run it. Hang with Braden, be a dad, take care of my parents. All the stuff that felt like a prison sentence before feels like freedom now. Everything's upside down, and the adventure is the prison. You know?'"

Her throat was choked with it. With J.J.'s pain, and Nate's. Her own felt very small and unimportant in comparison.

"I knew. I knew—"

A rift in his voice, and she knew he'd be silent until he could cover it, that he wouldn't cry for her, not now. When he was pulling away from her, telling her why this couldn't happen.

"I knew what it felt like to think your reasons were the right ones, or at least good enough, and to discover that—that they weren't. So I said—I said—*fuck*."

She put her arms around him, but he pulled away and put his self-control back on like a mantle, and said, "I said, A few more weeks, dude. Just hang in a few more weeks, and you'll be back there."

She could hear his breathing. Ragged. But she didn't touch him.

"Maybe it doesn't sound like much. But I feel like I lied to him. Like I promised him. And there are so many promises you can't keep. So—God, I don't know. I felt like there was this one I had left, and I had to keep it."

But you never promised him you'd do it if he couldn't! she wanted to cry. *You never promised you'd take his place!*

But she didn't. Even though she saw all the twists in his logic. All the peculiar ways that what he was telling her didn't quite add up. How taking over the store and fathering J.J. and being a surrogate son to Braden's parents could never in a million years give J.J. or Braden or Jim or Suzy back what they had lost. Of course it couldn't. Just like it couldn't give Nate back J.J.

She stayed quiet, because he was telling her he'd lost something else, too. Some sense of being a man who could keep his word. Who could be counted on to mean what he said. He was telling her that there was a way he could have *that* back.

She couldn't take that away from him.

She couldn't ask him to break this one, last, promise.

"Do you—do you understand?"

Still, she couldn't quite answer.

Finally, "It's what you need to do. Of course I understand that."

And the look on his face. The gratitude. It made her sure she'd done the right thing. And then the gratitude transmuting gradually into something else. Something greedy. Her body already primed to answer.

"Will you do something for me?"

She nodded. *Anything.*

"Will you tell me what you want? I want to hear you ask for it." That look in his eyes, that dark look so she knew exactly what he meant.

She hesitated. Nodded.

It was like being onstage at first. The words coming jolting and awkward. "I want . . . Nate, I can't—"

"You can."

Then, because he wanted it, because he'd asked for it, "Kiss . . . me. The . . . those . . . little kisses."

She could drown in the sensations—the heat of his mouth, the nip of his lips and teeth—and in the emotions. Her hunger. His. The recklessness. The sorrow.

And when he pulled away, the expression on his face. She would do anything to make him look at her like that. She would do anything for the gratitude and the desire.

"I want your tongue."

"Where?"

"In my mouth."

He obliged. Lingeringly. Obliterating thought for a long time.

"Where else?"

"Here." She showed him. "Here."

"And here?"

"Definitely there."

He groaned. When his tongue slid against hers. When his tongue flicked upward against her nipple. When his tongue slide down her ribs, tucked into her navel, found the matching heat between her legs. He groaned as if he were the one being touched.

That made it easier. It made it so easy. "Yes. Just like that." And, "Slower. *Slower.* Tease me."

And she could use her hands, too, to tell him, pulling him up to kiss her again, putting his hands where she wanted them, on her breasts, his fingertips against her face, hands grasping her waist, one hand cupping her greedy center, where heat had pooled and she'd melted into it.

"Rub. Like you did the other day. And touch my nipples."

Then, when neither of them could stand it any longer, and he was inside her, moving, when his heat was her heat and there was really no distinction at all, she could ask with her body, with her hips, with her rhythm. With her nails, with the sounds that were coming out of her without her meaning to make them, breath huffed against his ear, whimpers into his mouth, a moan against his collarbone. Pleas.

She asked and she asked and she asked, for touch after touch, for more, for faster, for deeper, but it was like that childhood Christmas-morning sensation, how she could never recapture the moment of pure possibility she'd felt when she first saw the riches, glimmering, glossy, bright. It was like how as the day wore on and bounty turned to excess and still nothing quite fed the ache, each additional gift became a taunt. Something else you'd have to find a place for, something else you could lose or break. And she was reaching, asking for more, using every word to try to tell him all these things she knew he wanted her to ask for, when inside there were so many things she wanted to ask for

Tell me how much you need me.

Tell me you could change your mind.

Tell me you know this is a kind of promise, too.

But she couldn't, wouldn't, say it, the words drifting away like smoke.

He stroked into her, his pace perfect, steady, speeding only a little as his eyes dropped closed and his body stiffened and the wedge of his hips against her sex pushed her over the edge.

"I want . . . I want . . ."

But she couldn't find it. She had the shape and the texture, but not the name.

23

"Thanks for holding down the fort."

She nearly screamed, startled by the unexpected appearance of a six-foot-plus ex–Army Ranger outside her PT office. Jake.

He came inside and sat on the counter. He looked tired, but not too strung out. That was a good sign, surely?

"Sorry—I probably should have texted you I was back."

"No, it's okay. I'm glad you're back. I take it this means your mom is okay."

"She's doing great. And my sister's there. I'm going to go down this weekend for a half-day each day to help out, but I thought given how long I was away, it would probably be a good idea to get my ass back in here."

So it was a lucky thing, after all, that Nate had come back last night to claim his bonus time. Because she wouldn't have wanted not to have that time with him. As much as she hurt now, she wouldn't have wanted to miss out on a minute of it. Not only because of how good it had felt, how purely pleasurable and how deeply liberating. But also because she had learned so much from him. About herself. About what she wanted. And that would go with her wherever she went, even if last night had been the end for them.

Strange how something could feel so unfinished and yet so *over*. When he'd said goodbye to her at the door of her room this morning, a slow, final kiss, his hands slipping out of hers, his body drawing back from hers, opening a cold space between them that widened until the door closed, so quietly, behind him.

"I'm glad you're back. Because I'm going to go back to Seattle. At least for a little while. Until—"

There was no point in beating around the bush now, right? There was nothing to protect.

"Until Nate leaves."

Jake's expression barely changed. She hadn't surprised him.

"You knew!"

He shrugged.

"You knew I was full of it when I said nothing else was going to happen with him."

"Not that you were full of it. It wasn't you that clued me in. I mean, I suspected. But it was Nate who gave it away, actually. He was so pissed at me when I tried to call him off you. I figured if you were just anyone to him, he'd have laughed the whole thing off."

On a better day, that revelation might have meant something to her. She wasn't *just anyone* to Nate. But it was small consolation right now, when last night he'd told her he didn't want to stop seeing her but that he was going to, anyway. And why.

"It's not—it's not going to happen."

Now Jake looked surprised. He shifted awkwardly, then said, "Sometimes it's the right thing at the wrong time. I have some experience with that."

She didn't know all the details of Jake's life before he'd lost his leg and left the Army, but she did know that even though Jake and Mira had been together only a handful of years, Sam was Jake's son. So there had been a *wrong time* for them.

"I think we already had our wrong time," she said. "I think this is our right time—it's just more of a *right now* kind of right time."

"Are you sure?"

Nate's words. *There are so many promises you can't keep . . . There was this one I had left, and I had to keep it.*

Several times during the night, wakeful in his arms, she'd thought about asking if she could go with him. But she hadn't. Because he'd been dead right. There was nothing for her in Eagle Hill, nothing but feeling pathetic because she'd let a man pull her away from her own goals. And she'd also understood what he hadn't said, that there were some kind of promises that took up all your emotional energy. That prohibited you from making another promise until you had fulfilled them. In the end, she'd been glad she'd kept her mouth shut—and her pride intact.

She nodded. "Yeah. I'm sure."

"So you're going to leave. Until Nate does."

"Yeah."

"No," a voice said from the doorway. "You stay. I'll leave."

He looked good. Relaxed, nonchalant, the way you'd expect a man who'd gotten laid to his heart's content to look.

And sure of himself in a way she hadn't seen since—since the Becca days. The old Nate.

It hurt. She wouldn't have thought there was much worse hurting to be done, but the fact that he'd said it so baldly, and in front of Jake—it meant it was really over. Up till this point she'd been able to hold on to a faint hope that Nate would protest the idea of a separation when it came down to it, but here he was. *You stay. I'll leave.* Not looking like his heart was breaking, like hers.

And the chivalry of it, the fact of what he was doing, trying to save this situation for her, that hurt, too. Because he was such a good, gentle, generous man. Because—as she always had—she *loved* him.

She couldn't look at him, at his golden hair, at the body she'd had under her and over her and every way she'd asked for, at the hint of mischief she remembered from the old days lurking behind his eyes.

Most of all, she couldn't look into those eyes, because no matter what she saw there, it would hurt worse.

"I have to leave anyway," she told him. "I can't stay here. Not after—"

She looked to Jake for confirmation, but his eyes were on Nate.

"You're sure you're ready, man? You were in bad shape three weeks ago."

"I've been handling it. I did some kayaking with Braden while I was down there, and a couple times, yeah, it hurt, but I dealt with it. Li taught me good tricks."

There was no wink-wink, nudge-nudge behind his words, and that hurt, too. He was being careful with her.

"What's been working best?"

"Mental stuff helps. Relaxation, focus, all that. It's not like a magic cure, but I feel more on top of it."

His eyes found hers, then. Damn the gratitude in them. Damn him for being a fast learner, for being determined, for being tough. For being the kind of guy who didn't really *need.*

"Does that work for you, Li? He goes, you stay?" Jake crossed his arms.

"Seriously? After I waltzed over the ethical line and then betrayed your trust?"

"You told me at the first possible opportunity, in each case, yes?"

"I could have told you on the phone yesterday morning."

He laughed. "Then I probably would have told you to go to hell. Good for you for waiting till I had a clearer head."

"But I—"

"You told me you had a conflict. We straightened it out. Now you've got another issue—"

He looked to Nate as if expecting an argument from him, but when he didn't get one, he continued: "And you're offering me a solution to that, as well. All I see here is a good problem-solver."

And, she reflected bitterly, a woman who would be jobless as well as heartbroken if Jake weren't generous enough to keep her on, even though she'd done everything she could to screw things up.

Jake's charity hurt, too.

"I found a couple donors, enough to pull together a pretty darn decent salary for you," Jake said. "So if you still think R-and-R could be the right place for you—I've got a job for you."

She let herself look at Nate. He was beaming. So pleased for her. So sure she'd been given exactly what she wanted.

Three weeks ago, this *would* have been exactly what she wanted.

After all, she'd said it herself, in the beginning. The goal had always been to make him not need her anymore.

24

"You *bastard*."

Alia had left, and Jake's fists were clenched tight. Nate thought Jake was going to throw a punch. Knock him against a wall.

"You selfish bastard. I told you to leave her alone. I told you not to mess with her head."

If it had been only Jake's rage, even the threat of violence, Nate would have taken what was coming to him. But the way Jake was painting Alia, like she'd had no agency at all, like she had no idea what she wanted—he couldn't stand it.

"Don't you dare make her a victim. You're not her big brother. She's not some helpless—you don't know a thing about it."

Startled, Jake released his fists and took a step back.

"I did the best I could. I don't owe you an apology and I don't owe you an explanation."

"No, but you owe her *both*."

He thought of last night. He hadn't apologized, and he

didn't think she would have wanted him to. He couldn't be sorry. Not for any of it. Not for one single second of what had passed between them, and even less as time had gone on and she'd opened herself more fully to him. He could never be sorry for the last two days, especially for the sexting, for the way she'd slowly showed him what she wanted, told him what she'd needed. He couldn't be sorry for having been right about *MenInUni242,* who had been there all the time, all Alia, waiting for him to invite her out to play.

And he *had* explained. He'd explained the best he could, and she'd listened, the way she always listened, and she'd understood, the way she always understood. The way she had in the letters, before he'd known it was her. Before he'd known she was real.

"What I owe her is between her and me. Did she tell you I'd messed with her head?"

Jake shook his head. "No."

"Did she tell you she thought I was unfair to her? That I used her?"

"No."

I rest my case.

He turned to go.

"Hey," Jake said.

Nate turned back.

"I just don't want you to make the same mistake I made," he said.

"What, getting a chick pregnant and then abandoning her for the next seven years?"

Jake held up his hands. "Okay. Okay. I deserved that."

"No," Nate said with a heavy sigh. "You didn't."

"I don't want you to lose years of your life you could have because you're ... because you're afraid."

Nate shook his head. "I think you have it all backward," he said. "I'm not afraid of her. Being with her is—"

Last night she'd told him everything she'd wanted. One after another, the requests, the demands, falling like Seattle rain, surrounding him like a mist, all his senses tuned.

Do this.

Give me.

Like this.

I want ...

"—the sweetest, least threatening thing there is. It would be the easiest thing in the world to—"

To let myself love her.

"—just throw in my lot with her. But I can't. I can't do that. I've got things I have to do."

"Things you *think* you have to do."

"Things I know I have to do," Nate said. "Things I'd hate myself if I didn't do."

"You might hate yourself if you don't give this a chance."

"I'm not you, and she's not Mira. What you wanted to do and what you needed to do were the same thing. That's not true for me. If I stay here for her, I will always know I made the selfish choice. And I will never be whole. And that's no basis—for anything. Like trying to build a skyscraper on a bad foundation."

Jake turned toward the window, then back. Ran a hand through his hair. Then said, "You're right. You're right. I'm making assumptions. I'm making assumptions because of my own situation. And that's not fair. I'm sorry. And you're right

—she never said any of those things. That you treated her badly or any of that."

Nate knew she hadn't. That she wouldn't have.

Here.

Slower.

Tease me.

Touch me.

Now, now, now.

It had been everything he'd hoped for, and yet—

When she'd emptied herself of everything, when she'd begged him for what she needed, there had been one thing missing.

All those wants, golden things to behold, under his skin, in his ears, filling all his senses, all those things she'd asked for, and she'd never once asked the one he'd most dreaded— and most hoped for. The request he would never have been able to refuse, the plea that would have swept away duty.

Please stay.

UNTIL HE'D APPEARED in Jake's office, she'd held out hope that he would change his mind. That by some miracle when she opened herself completely to him, when she asked him for all the things she had wanted but not been able to speak aloud, he would realize that he had fallen in love with her and that managing a hardware store and tending to another man's family was not, in fact, as important to him as she was.

But that hadn't happened.

And now she knew it wasn't going to.

She was so far inside her own head, so hurt and sad, so worn out from the day's honest work and what the last forty-eight hours had put her through, that she almost tripped over her own sister.

Becca was sitting with her back against the door to Alia's room, her knees pulled up, waiting.

No.

Instant guilt. She'd never had a *no* in her heart for her sister. Never. Not once. Not through all the days and weeks, stretching into months and years, that she'd been Becca's parent.

But she was so tired. So hurt. She wanted to crawl into her bed and pull the covers over her head and—

She didn't think she even had the energy to cry. Not now, not yet. Maybe soon. Maybe when the exhaustion wore off and she remembered the good moments, when Nate was gone from R&R and she began to register his absence. When she began to reckon up what she'd had and lost and had and lost again.

"What are you—what are you doing here? And how did you know where to find me?"

"Someone named—Gabi?—gave me your room number. She's very friendly."

Ah, Gabi.

"I can leave—"

Her face must have looked as unwelcoming as she felt, and reflexively she pulled her mouth into a smile, even though she knew it probably wasn't reaching her eyes. "No. Of course you won't leave. Come in."

"I—I had to get out of Seattle. It felt claustrophobic."

Becca was on the brink of tears. And Alia—with a surge of relief—felt that strange gratitude rising in her, the pleasure of being able to draw her sister to her feet and put both her arms around her. The familiar warmth, the home scent of Becca's hair, the way hugging family felt different and more comfortable than any other contact.

She led Becca into her room and switched on the electric kettle to make them cups of tea and straightened the bedclothes without letting herself think about why they were so rumpled. And then the two of them curled up on the bed.

"What happened, baby?"

Tears spilled over from Becca's eyes, and her face crumpled.

"That bad, huh?"

"I called him. I told him I was so sorry and I wanted to talk about it. I asked him if he'd come over."

"Good for you, hon!"

But she already knew where this was going. The sight of Becca leaning against her door had told her everything she needed to know about the outcome.

Sometimes talking about it only made the fundamental problems more clear. It brought undercurrents to the surface.

"He came over. He was so nice, Li. I think that's the worst part. He was *so* nice. He said he totally accepted my apology and we all have those moments when we want to flee. And he listened so patiently to what I was telling him."

It is worse when they're nice. When they listen and under-stand, but tell you, in the end, that they don't love you. Not enough, anyway.

"I basically told him the whole history. How things were really chaotic when we were kids and no one caught the fact that I was struggling so badly in school. I said I'd always thought of myself as stupid, and that when I saw his books, and he said what he said, I freaked out."

Becca was still teary, but her voice had gained strength as she talked.

"I'm proud of you, Bex," Alia said. "That couldn't have been easy."

Becca shook her head. "It wasn't some big heroic thing. I just—I just felt like it was my last chance with him, you know? I was laying my cards on the table."

Yeah, I know, Alia thought. And it hadn't been any act of heroism for her, either, telling Nate how she felt about it. Just the words that had come out when it was time for truth-telling. *I don't want to stop. Doing this. Being with you.*

"He told me he really appreciated my honesty. He said something like what you just said, that it couldn't have been easy telling him that whole story, and he respected me for doing it. But I could see it. On his face. That there was a big ol' 'but' coming. And sure enough—" She hesitated. "You probably think I'm an idiot. For even caring. It was four dates, right?"

She shot an appealing glance in Alia's direction.

Alia shook her head. Touched her sister's soft blond hair. "I think you can tell a lot about someone in a short time."

"I know, right? I think—"

Becca closed her eyes and put her hands over her face.

"I think I was probably already in love with him."

Me, too.

She almost said it. But then Becca began to cry, hard, racking sobs that pulled up from the root of her, and Alia knelt up and crawled to her, put her arms around her. "Shh, hon. You're all right."

She held her for a long time, until Becca's sobs subsided. Inside her own chest, her own grief was held back and frozen —still and heavy.

She thought of telling Becca the whole story. It might feel good to let it spill, after all this time. How she and Nate had gotten together, how sex had spun itself into intimacy, into a closeness so deep and thorough that it hurt now to be deprived of it. How she had hoped, how she had given everything she had, how it hadn't been enough. But Becca felt so good in her arms, a reason to put one foot in front of the other, someone to take care of, to comfort, to pour herself into. Her story could wait until Becca felt better. Until the storm had passed.

"He said things in his life were complicated. And he wanted to be honest with me now so he wouldn't hurt me later. He said he didn't have the time or the energy for complicated, and that obviously I was complicated, which wasn't a bad thing, just not—not *his* thing, not *right now.* Right now, he needed simple. And that he was sorry. Really, really sorry. Sorry he hadn't been honest with me sooner, before we'd—" In an uncharacteristically violent move, she slammed her fist down into the bed. And then again, until Alia took her hand and held it fast in her own, a trembling thing. "I wish I hadn't. You told me to be careful—"

"You didn't do anything wrong. You slept with a guy you liked. That's not a crime. And what happened wasn't punishment. It was just—it was just two people going in different directions."

Becca's hand had stilled. Her shoulders had slowed their

shaking, and when she looked up at Alia next, her face was calmer.

"You don't need him," Alia said.

She'd said it as much to herself as to Becca, and with far more certainty than she felt. While her chest felt like concrete, faulty with cracks.

25

"Grab your balls."

Alia used that phrase frequently because they all found it so entertaining, because she had learned with time that the dirty jokes and crotch-hoisting that followed her command were as therapeutic as the varied-size bright-colored rubber balls the men used for the next set of exercises.

There were ten vets, now, in Alia's class, and even though almost every man arrived at his first class full of certainty that it was a waste of time, almost all of them returned. She'd even gotten an email from a "graduate" who reported taking Pilates classes in the "real" world. *It's all women in the class, but I figure you can't claim to be much of a soldier if you get intimidated by a roomful of chicks.*

She should feel great about what she'd accomplished. She should feel only joy at how much she'd helped these guys.

But there was a bleakness to it all for her. A sense of trudging through routine. In some ways, not so terribly different from the way she'd felt in her old job, as if the buzz of *doing the right thing* was somehow out of reach.

Even though Jake had made it more than clear how much he valued her. Even though he'd promised her that in a few weeks he'd be able to begin paying her a small salary. He'd even set aside time each day when neither of them had appointments so they could share successes, get each other's help with issues, and trade techniques and knowledge.

None of that filled the hole Nate had left behind.

With a heavy heart, she led them through the ball routine —small green balls with divots under their feet, medium-size orange balls under their shoulder blades and then under their hips, the big blue ball braced behind them for crunches. And then they draped themselves over the gigantic exercise balls and lay there, contemplating the opening of their vertebrae, and she had a moment to reflect.

The night Becca had arrived, the two of them glommed popcorn and therapeutic milkshakes and mourned, Becca openly and Alia in secret. *I'll tell her tomorrow,* she'd thought. *Or—in a few days. When she's feeling better. When I'm feeling better.*

Because, right then, she worried that without the pleasures of feeding and comforting, without the distraction of bustling around making things okay for Becca, in much the way she always had, she would fly apart into a million pieces.

If she told her secret, if she told her story, she would be the one who needed to be taken care of, and that—

It would be like it had been that night, the night of the instant messages. Her gone all to pieces, Becca doing the taking-care-of.

She couldn't imagine it. Not right now.

Two days after that, Nate had left.

He'd come to her office beforehand. To thank her, he said, which he did with a strange formality. "You helped me so much. I can't tell you how grateful I am." Shaking her hand, but not quite meeting her eyes. Even that contact felt good, as good as foreplay, her body declared, but she shushed it.

She hoped—she hoped he'd say something else. *I won't forget you.* Or maybe—this was a wild dream, but, maybe—*I hope I'll see you again sometime.* But if there were words left between them, he didn't utter them. Neither did he linger or cast her a longing backward glance. He just said, "Bye, Alia," and went next door, where she heard him say exactly the same things to Jake in a slightly warmer tone of voice. And then she heard their amiable laughter and chatter, and she was beyond grateful when Griff came into the office and threw himself down on the table with a grunt of pain.

When Griff had gone, she'd watched from the window as Nate loaded the truck, muscles bunching under his shirt across his broad back as he hoisted a bag in. He wrestled playfully with the guys who came down to see him off. He smiled and laughed and punched arms and accepted manly hugs, and if she hadn't been so sad for herself, she would have been filled with joy for him, because he seemed so *whole.* So *him.*

And then he was gone. She thought maybe he'd look once in her direction, betray some wistfulness, but he never did.

"Um, do you want us to go over the ball forward, too?" a deep voice asked.

She'd left them draped on their backs over the ball during that whole reverie. She hoped none of them would suffer irrevocable spinal damage. "Yes, definitely, sorry," she said, and they all changed position obediently. That was the nice thing about soldiers. Once they'd decided you were indeed ahead of them in the chain of command, they were pretty good about following instructions.

Alia's phone buzzed. Becca.

Are you coming back here after class?

Y.

She remembered what that single letter had signified to Nate, and her face got hot, her body loosening in habitual anticipation. And then sadness settled over her again, washing away desire.

Good—need to talk.

She cheered a little at the sight of that. It had been such a boon, the ability to bury her own feelings in the experience of taking care of Becca.

"Actually, let's say we're done for today," she told the men. She usually ran the class past its official stop time and up to mere seconds before her first appointment of the day, but she —she didn't have it in her today. She wanted to slink off somewhere and lick her wounds. Or administer to Becca's, anyway.

"Feel free to stay there as long as you need to." She paused for effect. "Put your balls away when you're done."

Snickers from the peanut gallery, but even that couldn't eke a smile out of her.

"JAKE TOLD ME."

They were the first words out of Becca's mouth when she opened the door to admit Alia.

"Told you what?"

Alia wasn't being cagey. She was startled, still in the teaching zone, and vague-brained with grief. For that moment, at least, she had absolutely *no* idea what her sister could possibly be talking about.

"That you were dating Nate. That he broke up with you. Alia—I don't understand. I don't—"

Her voice broke off, one hand in mid-flail.

Oh, *shit.*

"Bex—"

"Jake didn't mean to tell me, he figured I'd know, because, yeah, *duh,* sisters usually tell each other this stuff." She crossed her arms. "When Jake said it—'Is she okay? Because I'm pretty sure she's more upset than she lets on, I think they were pretty serious'—I was like *Whaaa?* Then he refused to tell me anything, but I kind of figured it out. Or the gist. You didn't—you didn't think I'd freak out, did you?" Becca narrowed her eyes.

"No. No!"

"I would have thought, with the whole history, with me knowing what happened in the past, you would have been dying to tell me. It's not like you can say, 'Oh, it was so complicated, I didn't want to get into it.' So why? Why?" Becca's face sagged, and Alia realized that all her anger up to that point had been bravado. Her sister was near tears. Hurt.

She'd hurt Becca.

And that was it. There was nothing left but the whole damn story, and it was time. It was long past time.

Alia took a deep breath. Squared her shoulders. Maybe she could do this. Just tell the story, one word after another:

"In the beginning, I kept trying to deny that it was happening at all—"

"Because he was a client." Becca lifted her chin. Just a little, but it eased Alia's heartache.

"Yeah. I knew I wasn't supposed to be attracted to him. So at first I didn't tell you because I hoped there was nothing to tell."

"And the other day on the phone, I blabbed too much and didn't even ask you how you were. I didn't leave you any time to talk."

"No!" That was Becca all over, eager to make this about her own failings, and Alia couldn't let her. "It wasn't that. I knew you would have listened if you knew I needed you to. I did. I just—I didn't tell you because I knew if I did, I'd—"

To Alia's horror, her voice cracked, and the tears she'd been holding in threatened to spill. She swiped them away.

"I knew I'd start crying," she finished. "And then you'd feel like you needed to comfort me."

"What's so terrible about that? I cry all the time to you. I was crying the other night. We could have cried together. We could have drowned our sorrows jointly in alcoholic pepper-mint milkshakes. Which, by the way, need a name."

"But that's not how it is with us," Alia protested.

"I know." Becca's voice was suddenly quiet. Her face sad. "I know that's not how it is. You don't tell me things. You don't cry with me."

The accusation twisted in Alia's chest, more painful because she knew it was true.

"That one time you did—then you wouldn't ever talk

about it again, and I never wanted to bring it up. If I even hinted around it, you'd get all . . . stiff—"

They both knew what *one time* Becca was talking about. And Alia didn't even try to deny what her sister was saying, because it was painfully true. She'd felt stiff, rigid and miserable, every time the conversation had wandered back there, to that epic meltdown.

"But what I *don't* understand is *why.*"

Because when you were the one who always took care of someone, it was hard to let them take care of you. Because she had been watching out for Becca for so long that she didn't remember how *not* to, which meant she didn't remember how to ask her for help. Because the one time she'd needed help she'd felt like she was breaking into a thousand tiny pieces, like if she let that happen she would never put herself back together again.

"I guess it's—bad habit."

Alia sat down heavily on the bed. Becca pulled the desk chair out and sat down across from her. Waiting, listening, so intently it made Alia uncomfortable. She had to look away. "I've always—I've always taken care of *you.*"

"Because you think of me as the baby."

"No!"

"Because of my disability."

"Becca, *no.*"

"Then I don't understand. Because it's fine for me to need you, right, but you can't need me. God forbid *you* ever need taking care of. God forbid you ever let anyone help you with anything. It's so damn frustrating. You're my *sister.* I love you. And I want us to be friends. I don't want you to mother me or take care of me, I just want you to be my friend."

"Of course I'm your friend!"

"But I'm not yours. I'm not *your* friend, because if I was your friend, you would have told me what was going on in your life."

The truth hung in the air between them.

And then Becca bowed her head. "I'm sorry," she said. "This is the last thing you need, me yelling at you. This isn't how I wanted this to go. I just—Li, you can't give and give and give until you have nothing left to give. At some point you have to take what you need for yourself. Otherwise you end up with nothing to give. Otherwise, you end up with nothing."

Alia thought of the last night she and Nate had been together. How he'd made her ask for what she needed. How hard it had been at first, a skill she'd never possessed, and how it had grown easier, until the words had poured from her, all that *want* finally unleashed. And how there had been one more thing she had wanted that she hadn't been able to tell him.

Maybe if she had been able to—maybe things would have gone differently.

"I'm not very good at—"

He'd said it himself, hadn't he? *You're not very good at saying what you want, are you?*

"I'm not very good at needing things." The words came easily, as if the confession had been waiting to emerge all this time, and then more easily, faster now: "I'm not good at needing *people.* I'm not very good at letting people love me. And I'm sorry, Bex," she said, starting to cry. "I'm so, so sorry I didn't let you be my friend."

She cried for a long time, while Becca held her.

When Alia's sobs had turned to hiccups and her hiccups to ragged breaths, Becca said, "I'm so lucky."

"What—"

"I always had you," Becca said, very softly. "You saved me. You took care of me. You made everything okay. You didn't have that."

Alia shook her head. "No. I didn't."

"Dad was gone. Mom wasn't—*there.*"

They were both quiet for a moment, remembering *those* years—the drawn shades, chores undone, but, worst of all, the silences.

"It must have been hard for you. Taking care of me. Rescuing me from myself."

"No. It was never hard. Loving you was never hard. But this—"

God, the words just didn't want to come out. The admission of vulnerability. How much of a shell had she built so she would never have to need this? "This thing. With Nate. And now."

"Letting people take care of you."

Alia nodded. Because she had never, ever, ever wanted to screw up and make Becca bail her out, the way their parents had made her bail them out; she had *never* wanted to do that to anyone.

"I'm grown up now." Becca didn't sound angry or defensive. It was just a simple statement of fact.

"I know you are."

"No, I mean—you can let me take care of you. A little. When you need it."

Tears rushed into her eyes, and Becca's surprisingly warm, strong arms were around her again, and it was a little easier than it had been last time to accept the sensation of falling apart.

They talked first about the past. Times when both her mother and father had sat on her bed to say good night. Times, even when her father had been ill, when he had had the time and energy to listen to her talk about school. To help her solve her problems, to sit with her while she plugged away at her math homework, to help her work out a passage on the piano. And later, those rare—but real—times when her mother's mood had been stable enough that she'd been a mother, someone who helped Alia pick out clothes, someone who did the grocery shopping and cooked dinner. Someone who was present and comforting, not a blank space in the house.

They had felt so few and far between, so unutterably precious, and so unrecoverable.

When both sisters had stopped crying for the second time, Alia told Becca about Nate, from the moment Jake had come to her to ask if she would be okay with treating him. She told Becca every detail she could without breaking therapist-patient confidentiality—and without making it TMI.

When Alia was done, Becca said, "When we first met him at the picnic. When you introduced him to me and walked away—"

"I never should have." Alia remembered the little flutter of panic, the faintest awareness, far under her skin, that he was something she wanted so badly that she couldn't let herself even think it. She had to push him away, fast and far, put him out of her reach before he could become yet another person who couldn't love her. "I pushed him away. I pushed him away so many times. And I don't know if it would have turned out any differently. It might not have. Because he was pushing me away, too—but maybe—if one of us had been able to be honest—"

She had come so close that night. So close to telling him the very most important thing.

"Do you think—" Alia began, then stopped.

She had never realized what a good listener Becca was, how quiet her face got, how her eyes held Alia's, warm and sympathetic.

Becca had always been ready to give Alia what she needed, if only Alia hadn't been so busy trying not to need anything at all.

"Do you think there's still a chance it's not too late?"

26

It had been only a couple weeks, but the more Nate got to know Jim, the more he admired him.

Everyone who came into the store and met Nate wanted to tell him how amazing Jim was, as if Nate couldn't see for himself.

The little old lady with her puffy gray hair pinned tight to her head wanted to know if Nate had heard the David and Goliath history of the store. Ten years ago, Yard & Home had opened less than five miles away, and everyone had predicted that Jim's store would be out of business within the year. But Jim hadn't been afraid. He'd shrugged and laughed it off. He'd quit selling lawnmowers, table saws, gas grills—the kinds of things he could never compete with Y&H over—and focused on what he knew he could do well. He offered repairs and advice, hiring even more salespeople with specialized plumbing, electric, and carpentry expertise. And he started selling specialty items: colorful wrapping paper, candles, perfume, local apparel, housewares.

His sales went up, not down, and after a while, he became

the place Y&H referred customers to for repair and installation help.

Nate had made all the appropriate noises, because it really was a terrific story, and because the little old lady's crush on Jim was totally adorable.

You only had to watch Jim work for a few days before you realized what kind of guy he was. The kind of guy *everyone* liked. The kind of guy who dispensed not only nuts and bolts, but also life advice. The kind of guy who was equally unfazed telling you how to install a toilet, how to help your kid build his Eiffel Tower project, and where to find a good divorce lawyer in town.

Watching Jim at work conferred the same kind of pleasure as watching an Olympic gymnast or figure skater. That pleasure you could take in watching someone do his job to the utmost, someone in the thorough flow of concentration.

For a day or so, Nate hoped that if he watched Jim long enough, he would have an epiphany about how much he wanted to be Jim when he grew up.

But instead, something else happened.

Watching Jim made him realize how much he wanted to do something he loved. Truly loved. Because watching someone work like that—watching someone do what he was clearly made to do—was a great thing.

He was envious of the joy Jim took in helping people, but that didn't make him want to sell them screws. It made him want to find the people he'd always wanted to help and help them the way he knew he could.

Just like Alia had said when he'd told her the plan to take over the hardware store. She'd reminded him of what it was he'd always said he wanted to do.

You said when you were out of the Army, you wanted to work with troubled teenagers. Because you almost weren't going to go to college at all, because of the money, and then that teacher—

She'd remembered, from the letters. She'd read, and she'd remembered, and when it had mattered, she had reminded him.

I'd be helping Braden, he'd responded to her.

But as he watched Jim with Braden, he wasn't so sure. The two of them, so alike, Jim leaning in close to instruct Braden in some detail of screen repair, or drilling Braden on customer service technique, or sitting down to their identical paper sack lunches, courtesy of Suzy. Nate had a sack lunch, too, and he often sat with them and ate. And they were always friendly and included him in whatever they were discussing, but—

He wondered.

He wondered if he was doing anyone any favors. Trying to *fill in* as if J.J.'s life were the sort of thing you could *staff*. What an absurd notion it seemed right now.

You couldn't pick up someone else's life as if it were something stray that had been cast aside. There was this alchemy to putting together a life, a blend of talent and passion that Jim seemed to have.

That Alia had.

He suspected it was part of what had attracted him so fiercely to Alia. The glow that lit her from within when she was doing what she loved, when she was standing over him on the table, telling him what was wrong and how she could fix it, when she was fixing it, her hands sure and professional on his body—

He made himself stop. There was nothing to be gained

anymore by thinking of her. It could only cause pain, a tightening in his chest that circled his ribs and caught him across the shoulder blade, that pulled at that unruly nerve in his neck until he had to go back into the storeroom and take a few minutes with the pain, which at least distracted him from the useless craving.

"Hey," Jim said. "You okay?"

He'd surprised him, coming up behind him.

"Yeah. I have this pain sometimes. From—"

They both knew what it was from.

"It used to be a lot worse, but I've been working with it, and it's getting better."

"You take breaks if you need breaks." Jim's hand, warm, a paw, on his shoulder.

Nate nodded, his chest tight with how much he wanted to be who Jim wished he were. How impossible that was.

He couldn't be anyone other than who he was. And he had to let Jim and Braden be who they were, too.

"Hey," Nate said. "I've been thinking about the kayaking trip."

A shadow passed over Jim's face, and Nate knew his intuition had been right.

"You should go with Braden. I'll watch the store."

He'd known, before he said it aloud, that it was the right thing.

The relief on the other man's face told him for sure.

THE PAIN GOT bad on the way home from the hardware store that day.

He knew it was his mind lashing out. Because the last little bit of certainty was gone now. There had been something he'd known he needed to do, and that had given him a reason. A reason to stop the pills, a reason to seek out Jake and healing, a reason to lay himself out and open on the table before Alia. *Here I am. Do your worst.*

But now the reason was gone, and the pain came back with a vengeance. And stayed.

On the second day, he called his doctor at the VA and asked him for another prescription. Drove himself to the pharmacy and picked it up. The bottle was in his pocket now, three days later, burning a hole there. He'd held on to it like a talisman. If the pain flared and spiked again, he'd take one. Just one.

So much easier than looking the pain in the eye, the way Alia had made him do. So much easier than looking into the void. Coming face to face with uncertainty.

Braden and Jim were gone, kayaking together somewhere on the Lower Owyhee. Nate was still staying with Suzy, though an apartment was opening up not too far from the store on the first of September, and he'd chatted informally with the landlord about taking over the lease.

Suzy had made pot roast and egg noodles for dinner, and she'd set the table as nicely as she did when everyone was there, even though it was only the two of them. She served him and then sat down, and then, as she always did, she asked how his day had gone and what crises he had had to avert in Jim's absence.

Nate was no Jim, but he could hold his own, make jovial conversation and comfort panicking divorcées who had depended on their husbands to mow the lawn, change the oil in the car, fix leaks, and replace lightbulbs. Nate was not even really in the hot seat, surrounded as he was by longtime employees who knew the store, and its loyal customers, better than he did. All he really had to do was work hard and follow instructions, both of which he was damn good at.

The only entertaining story he had from that particular day at work was the old guy who'd fought with him about which end of the hose was male and which was female. Finally Nate had to say, "Dude, it's just like *people*. Male goes into female."

To which the guy had said, "Oh. Well. It's been quite a while, for me."

He didn't feel like that was a story Suzy would appreciate. The person he *really* wanted to tell the story to was Alia.

He could text it to her.

But that would be unfair, just as it would have been unfair for him, at any point over the last week, to text her to tell her how much he missed her, how he was almost (but not *quite*) too unhappy to jerk off, how hard it was to make himself think of a generic, nameless woman when it was images of her that filled his head and hurt his chest.

He told Suzy another story instead, about a guy who'd needed help yesterday picking out a birthday present for his wife, and after much debate had chosen the most hideous scarf Nate had ever seen, despite three employees pointing him to numerous other choices. And then today the wife had come into the store with the scarf, and they'd all been certain she was going to exchange it, but instead she'd thanked them for helping him shop and said how much she loved it.

Suzy got tears in her eyes. "Aw. That is a great story."

Alia would love that story, too.

A wave of sadness passed over him. Someday, some other old guy would buy Alia a hideous scarf and she would think it was the most beautiful thing she'd ever seen. And she'd be the kind of woman who would go in and thank everyone in the store who'd helped her husband shop, too. Then she'd go home to her husband, who would definitely not *at all* appreciate her, and more to the point would have no idea how much strength and joy and *fire* were in her because she would never let him see it and he wouldn't know to ask—

He hadn't heard a word from her. Not that he was expecting her to beg him to change his mind. And it would be hard, hard for both of them to accept crumbs, text messages and letters, when they'd had *everything* for that short time. So maybe it was for the best that the end had really been the end.

Suzy put her hand over his. "Nate."

He looked at her. At the grief that had etched lines deep into her face. He hadn't known her before J.J.'s death, but he could imagine some of those lines away and see the woman Jim had married. The mother J.J. had grown up with. Calm, efficient, loving.

"What happened with her?"

"With who?"

"The one you were texting with last time you were here. The one who's made you so sad."

"She didn't do anything to make me sad."

She hadn't. She'd only done things to make him feel better. To feel *amazing.* And happy. Happy at a time in his life when he hadn't really expected that happy was a thing he could ever feel again.

"But you're—not with her anymore?"

He shook his head.

It was her eyes that got to him. Suzy's infinitely sad, infinitely wise, gray eyes. Staring into his like some ancient oracle.

"You know how grateful we are. For everything you've done for us. For helping out. For being J.J.'s friend."

"It's for me, too," he said. "It's something I want to do."

"Is it?"

Unwavering, those eyes. And under the scrutiny, he faltered a little, and she saw it.

"Nate. We love you like family. And if you want to stay here, you will always be welcome. Always. But—"

Something cracked behind her expression, a split second before she put it all back together again and smiled at him. Not a smile that traveled all the way into those troubled gray eyes, but a smile nevertheless.

"If you were my son—"

Which you will never be.

Because no one can bring J.J. back.

Because there are some promises that are never spoken aloud, but are broken anyway, and when those promises are broken, they can't be unbroken, no matter what we do.

"If you were my son, I would want you to be happy. I would—I would want you to live the life you were meant to live."

And really what we have to do is unbreak ourselves.

He touched the container in his pocket again.

27

Dear Nate,

    If I could do it over again, this is the letter I would write you.

This is me. Me, Alia, not me trying to win you over for Becca. Not me trying to help you feel better. Not me trying to fix you up or put you back together. Not trying to change your mind about where you are or what you need to do. Just me. Loving you.

When I saw you standing there at the picnic I wanted you for myself. I wanted you to love me. But wanting people to love me has never worked really well for me, so I decided not to want that. I introduced you to Becca instead, because I knew she was lovable because I loved her myself.

When I saw you kayaking on the lake at R&R I still wanted you to love me. And because of what I'd done to screw everything up, it still seemed even more unlikely that you ever would. So I decided to take the consolation prize I have always taken in situations like these. I decided I could be happy if you needed me. And for a while, I was happy with that.

But you taught me that I am allowed to ask for things. I am allowed to want things. I am allowed to say out loud the things I want.

When we were having sex the other night and you kept telling me to tell you what I wanted, I told you everything except the most important thing. I guess I've been holding back bits and pieces of myself all along. Hiding behind Becca, and just plain hiding. But here it is, what I didn't say. All the rest of me:

I want you to love me. Because I love you.

Love,

Alia

"I shouldn't have sent it through the mail. I should have sent it by email so at least I'd know for one hundred percent sure that he got it and is currently ignoring it. This is torture."

Becca tilted her head to one side. "Really? That would make you feel better? At least this way you can tell yourself—with no bullshit—that it has to have taken at least two days to get there and it will take at least two days for his response to come back."

But a response back in the mail wasn't the way Alia had pictured it. Even though she had wanted to be low-key and sensible and realistic about the whole thing, Alia now had to admit to herself that she had pictured him getting the letter and tearing it open. Reading it through in a burst of barely contained excitement. Tying his shoes, shouting over his shoulder to Suzy and Jim that he would be back but that he had to drive *right now* to R&R because he had something very, very important to do. Showing up at her door with his arms thrown wide—

That had been an egotistical fantasy. A fantasy that had

assumed that Nate was idling in Oregon, waiting only for Alia to come to her senses and claim him, and then he would abandon the mission that had driven him since coming home from Afghanistan and realize that all along he had loved her too much to leave her.

When really her letter had been all about her. About *her* owning the mistakes she had made, about *her* taking enough of a chance *on herself* to be willing to ask for love she hadn't somehow earned.

Writing the letter had been the right thing even if he never wrote back. She had to remember that.

"I don't want to go," Becca said. She was layering her things into her suitcase. She'd stayed a long time, explaining that now it was her turn to take care of Alia and she wanted to do it right. And she'd done a good job, although Alia had sometimes secretly laughed at what *taking care of* seemed to entail in Becca's mind. A lot of alcohol and sugar and earnest speeches. Making Alia *talk about things,* which included a lot of rehashing of childhood wounds. And remembering the good times. Those times when they'd been part of a happy family. *Before.*

And those times, *after,* when they'd managed to make for themselves a very small but genuinely happy family. Those days as teenagers when they'd had breakfast for dinner and then gotten in Alia's big bed and talked too late, because Alia was taking a break from being the perfect mom to be just a kid, too.

Those were good times. Maybe not family road trips to the Grand Canyon, Mom and Dad spatting over driving directions, Dad buying too many T-shirts and insisting on too many stops at visitors' centers, Mom gently mocking behind his back and overspending on ebooks—but good times, nevertheless.

"I don't want you to go," Alia said.

"You wouldn't consider coming back to Seattle?"

Alia shook her head. It was definitely tempting. Becca was her only family, and it would be good to be closer to her. But R&R had gotten under her skin, and she couldn't walk away from it or the job she loved so much. "I belong here."

"And maybe Nate will come back here—"

Alia frowned. "Don't. It makes it worse."

"You can't give up on him so soon."

"I haven't given up. I'm just . . . I'm being realistic."

She helped Becca carry her suitcase down to the car, gave her a huge hug, and promised to visit soon.

"Very soon. Like not months, but weeks."

"Promise."

Then Becca was gone, and that was worse. Like she'd taken all her optimism with her, and now Alia had to face the truth.

There was no reply from Nate. There wasn't going to be any reply.

Her phone buzzed and she practically jumped out of her skin. Yanked her phone from her pocket—

Jake: *Can you come to the office?*

It was hard to breathe, the disappointment was so crushing.

"THERE'S A PACKAGE FOR YOU."

Jake indicated a good-sized brown cardboard box on the credenza in his office. He raised an eyebrow.

She crossed the room to peer at it. It was addressed to her in block handwriting, no return address. "Do you think it's from the Unibomber?"

Jake grinned. "Seems doubtful. Although it came overnight, so someone obviously wanted you to get it quickly. You don't have any enemies, do you?"

She shook her head.

"You going to open it?"

"I feel like I should use tongs. Gloves. I don't know."

He laughed. "You want me to open it?"

"No, I'm good. Wait, actually—do you have a knife?"

He pulled his penknife from his pocket and slit the packing tape that held the box shut. "I've actually got a patient now, so take it back to your office. I want to know what's in there, though."

"Okay."

She didn't lift the flaps and peer inside the box. Something in her wanted to prolong the moment. The hope—the hope that it had something to do with her letter. The hope that it had something to do with Nate.

She carried it into her office. The package was surprisingly heavy. She tried to guess, but couldn't. She folded back the box flaps. The box was crammed with balled-up newspaper, underneath which she discovered a number of items individually wrapped in blue tissue paper over bubble wrap.

That was how she'd wrapped the items in Nate's care package.

She tried to suppress the giddy joy rising in her chest, without success. It kept trying to surface and break, and she was grinning now, trying not to do that, either, because really, Nate didn't have a monopoly on blue tissue and bubble wrap, and the care package could be from anyone. Her mom (though her mom wasn't the care-package type). Becca (though Becca had been the one to claim that care packages weren't worth the trouble). An old patient wanting to thank her for a job well done.

But she had to admit no patient had ever sent her a care package.

She wanted so badly for it to be from Nate.

The items were numbered, numbers written on half-size index cards in black Magic Marker, taped to the tissue paper. On the back of the first half-card, it said—she had to work to make out the words in the scrawl—*This isn't the* real *beginning, but it was a new beginning.*

She peeled back the paper and bubble wrap to find a pair of water shoes and a photo, printed on plain paper, of a woman kayaking. On the back of the photo, he'd written, *I couldn't fit an actual kayak in the box.*

She laughed. Out loud. She could actually hear his voice when she read the words. She could feel him in the room. And her heart was so full it almost hurt, because a care package meant he'd gotten her letter and he hadn't crumpled it up and thrown it away. A care package meant he—

Well, it might not mean what she thought, right? It might just mean he'd wanted to be in touch . . .

She wasn't going to allow herself to hope for more. He hadn't come himself. He'd only sent objects. When she'd poured herself into that letter—

But there were those words, *a new beginning.* Surely he wouldn't have said that if—

And a care package. No way that was a coincidence, which meant it was meant to echo the one she'd sent him—

In the next tissue-and-bubble-wrap package, there was some kind of device, with a hook and a nubby ball—some kind of . . . *sex toy*? Well, that would indicate that he wasn't just being chummy, wouldn't it?

It's a tapper. An actual tapper, so you can reach back and tap behind your shoulder blades. Seriously, you can buy anything on Amazon. And I confess, I bought one for myself, too.

Okay, so not a sex toy. But kind of cool. No, really cool. She tried to picture how he'd found it. Had he typed "tapper" into Google? Or stumbled on it accidentally? It didn't matter, she guessed—either way, he had bought it and wrapped it up, thinking of her all the while.

The next item was a swimsuit. A sporty blue one-piece. One she definitely would have picked out for herself. The note inside said, *I wanted to get you a string bikini so next time we go swimming together it's way easier to get you naked. But I know this is more your style.*

Happiness fizzed in her chest. *Next time. Get you naked.* Not a casual, friendly sort of care package, not at all. A *care* package.

Now her heart was pounding, trying to escape the cage of her ribs, and she was breathing fast, like she'd run a race. Blood rushed in her veins, light and hot as smoke.

Suzy's homemade cookies. You're lucky I didn't eat them all before they made it in the box. I wanted to send Cow Chip cookies, but a) there are none in Oregon, and b) I didn't want to copy you.

A baseball scorecard. No, not just *a* baseball scorecard, but *the* baseball scorecard, the one she'd helped him fill out that day at the Mariners game. And packets of mustard, ketchup, and relish. *Because, and I quote, "That's how you eat a hot dog at a ballpark." I think I knew that day. I don't think it's 20/20 hindsight. I honestly think I fell in love with you while leaning over Becca. Probably not something I should admit. Possibly not very romantic. Don't tell her. But you know me well enough by now to know I'm more honest than romantic.*

He was, and she *loved* that about him.

And a hideous scarf.

Huh?

Her happy internal soundtrack ground to a halt with one of those record-scratching noises.

There was no note with the scarf.

She shook it out in case there were answers in there somewhere.

She examined the pattern, in case it had some significance, but she couldn't detect any. In fact, there was nothing good you could say about the textile design, except maybe that it seemed to have incorporated every possible type of floral and paisley in every possible shade and hue, and therefore got points for thoroughness.

"What, you don't like it?"

Nate stood in the doorway, tall, muscular, burnished, smiling. Looking every bit as beautiful and capable as he had that very first time she'd seen him. Intimidating, powerful, infinitely desirable—and for a moment her mind pulled away into that old place—*I want him too much*—

And then she hurtled across the room and into his arms, and he was kissing her and kissing her.

28

S he broke the kiss off when he slid his hands under her shirt. "I think it was probably implicit in my promise to Jake that there would be no happy endings in my office."

He laughed. And then his face got very serious. "How would you feel more generally about a happy ending?"

She was very slowly, very cautiously, allowing herself to believe in what was happening. The care package, his being here—

But she didn't want to misinterpret him now. Didn't want to read too much into the kidding around. Like thinking that by "happy ending" he meant *happily ever after.*

"Li. I love you. I can't help it. Because you're you and I can't get enough of you. And I missed you so much, and after I read your letter, I realized I've been hiding, too."

"Hiding?" That was the word that popped out of her mouth, which was crazy, because of all the amazing things he'd said, she should have responded to one of the other ones, but all she seemed to be able to do was ask this asinine question.

"You know. Like you said in your letter, that you were hiding behind Becca and then just plain hiding. I was, too. Hiding out. Wrapping myself up J.J.'s life. Because it felt wrong to be happy. It felt wrong to let myself have you. When —when he—"

"Shh."

"I don't cry," he lied. "Ever."

"I know."

"I'm not crying."

"I know."

He held her so hard it hurt her ribs, but she didn't care. At all.

"What are we going to do?" he asked her.

"What do you mean?"

"I don't want to take you away from this job. If it's what you want. But I do love you. And I would like to spend a lot more time with you. Like maybe all the time. Like maybe sleep in the same bed with you and wake up in the morning next to you and tell you everything that goes through my mind. Everything that happens."

She was flummoxed by happiness. Struck dumb. She opened her mouth, tried to gather her thoughts, closed her mouth again. Tried one more time: "But you have to take care of Jim and Suzy and Braden."

"No. I don't. That's what I mean about . . . about hiding. I wanted to think they needed me because then I would have somewhere to be and something to do and I wouldn't have to think about what it meant that I was going to have a life and J.J. wasn't. If I had *his* life—if I took care of the things he was supposed to be taking care of—then that would somehow be okay. But it's not. It's not, and I realized, Jim is Braden's dad. He doesn't need another dad. A kindly uncle, maybe, but not a dad. And—they're missing J.J., of course they are, they miss him like fury, but they're also *complete,* if that makes any sense at all."

It made perfect sense. "They love you. But they don't need you."

"Exactly."

Because that, she thought, *is what it means to love unselfishly.* "Well," she said. "Jake happened to mention to me that he's going to be hiring a director of aquatics and boating." She frowned. "But it's only a part-time position."

Nate grinned at her. "Perfect."

"Perfect?"

"That would give me time to work on starting up my non-profit."

"Your non-profit?" She was apparently going to repeat everything he said, because her brain was too muddled with happiness to do otherwise.

"The one where I match mentors with at-risk youth in rural areas to keep them from dropping out or getting into drugs."

"Nate!" she said. She threw her arms around him.

He whispered against her ear. "Thank you for knowing me, even when I was too messed up to remember who I was." He pulled back and looked at her face. "Are you crying?"

"In the best possible way."

His lips found hers.

She had forgotten a lot of important details in a week and a half. How hot his mouth felt on hers. How expertly he used his tongue. How he often seemed to have more than two hands. That sound, caught halfway between grunt and groan, that he made when she found him under the denim of his jeans.

The dark, covetous look in his eyes. And she had to admit it to herself, she would never not want him to need her like that. Never. She could be a little bit selfish about that.

She looked at her watch. "I have a client in three minutes. But I will meet you in my room in sixty-three and a half minutes."

How his fingers felt pushing her hair behind her ear, how his expression could change in an instant from ravenous to tender—and back again.

"Deal."

IT WAS different from every other time with her. He guessed each time would feel this way, something new, a set of revelations.

This was slow and sweet. No playing, no talking, because there were no games and nothing to say. Just two people who felt comfortable enough in each other's arms to come out from hiding.

There were kisses, blending into more kisses, and he'd missed this so much, kissing her, holding her, her body yielding against his, but strong, too, resistance in all the right places. The kisses softening so there were no distinctions, only mouths and tongues and then just heat and wet and pressure and he wasn't sure he'd ever felt so much like he wasn't a body with parts but a single glowing self. Although

—he wasn't going to get all sappy about it—he was a guy and that never-ending goddamn *demand* that drove him was still alive and well, and after a while of just kissing and touching her tenderly, he'd had about enough of that.

She had, apparently, too, because she'd managed to get one of his thighs between hers and was rubbing herself against it, and the little noises she was making into his mouth got deeper and huskier and more demanding, and he wasn't sure she had any idea what she was doing with her hands anymore. One of them was pulling his hair and the other was sliding into the waistband of his pants—

She resisted when he tried to put enough distance between them that he could peel her out of her clothes and get himself out of his own, almost tearing his T-shirt in the process. Between each item of clothing, she tugged him back into those deep, sweet kisses, whimpering each time he pulled away from her. He lifted her, set her on the bed, tried not to break the kiss as he flailed at the nightstand for a condom—

This time, she was the one to pull away. Breathless, eyes sleepy, face flushed, lips swollen. The curves of her body laid out before him like the best feast ever. *God,* she was gorgeous.

"I have an IUD. You don't have to do that. Assuming you're—"

"Clean." He'd already torn the packet open, and he looked at the thing with the loathing he always hid in a dutiful, gentlemanly way, and then threw it gleefully across the room and grinned at her. "I've never done it without a condom."

"Me neither."

He was worried about his staying power, because right

now it felt like he'd go off the second he got inside her, or maybe before if he didn't hurry the hell up.

But as it turned out, that wasn't a problem. Because once he was inside her all he wanted to do was stay there as long as he possibly could. To be in her, on her, over her, raised up on his arms so he could stare into her eyes, watch them go all cartoon-spirally when he thumbed her nipples and slid a hand down to find her swollen clit, all the while marveling at how hot and tight and sweet she was, how he could go all night like this, the perfect rhythm, long strokes, filling her completely and watching her eyes close in bliss—

Well, he *could* have gone all night, except then she clutched him and lifted her hips suddenly and made an *oh!* sound of surprise, her body clenching around his, her head thrown back, her mouth open, and she was so unrestrained, so unhidden from him, the way she thrashed under him, her face screwed up with it, that he gave up and poured himself into her.

Later, his arm tight around her, she said, "You still didn't explain about the scarf. I get all the rest of it. But not the scarf."

As they lay there quietly together, he told her all the stories of the last couple weeks. What it had been like to see Jim doing his job, the Olympic champion of hardware-store ownership and unexpected fatherhood tinged with tragedy. How Nate had given the kayaking trip back to Jim and Braden, whose trip it always should have been. How he'd gotten the oxy prescription and kept it in his pocket. What Suzy had said to him at the dinner table, about living the life he was meant to live.

About how he had gotten up from the table, his hand in

his pocket, and gone to the bathroom. Broken the seal, opened the bottle, dumped the pills into the toilet. Flushed and walked away without looking back.

She just grinned at that, and nodded. Like, *Of course you did. I never had any doubt.*

And he told her the other stories, too. The smaller ones he'd wanted to be able to tell her as they happened. Including the customer arguing passionately (and incorrectly) about the male and female hose ends.

She laughed out loud, and *man,* that was what life was about. Making Alia laugh.

Finally, he told her the scarf story. The poor misguided bastard with his horrible scarf choice, and how it had turned out, after all, that the scarf had been an act of love and understanding. And how much Nate had wanted to tell Alia. How much he'd wanted to tell her—

He hesitated. It felt like a lot. Maybe too much.

"No hiding," she said.

He nodded. "No hiding," he agreed.

So he told her. How he'd thought about there being another guy someday, that guy and Alia grown old together, and how that guy would be the one to give her the scarf, and how Nate couldn't stand it because he knew no one would ever do as good a job of knowing her as he could do. As he wanted to do.

"Oh," she said, the same sort of pleasure and surprise in her voice that had been in it when he'd unexpectedly made her come. "Well. I don't *want* anyone else to know me like you do."

"And then it seemed obvious that I needed to send the care package."

"You mean after you got my letter."

"No. I sent the care package before I got your letter."

She wrinkled up her nose, looking adorably confused. "But you said after you read my letter you realized—"

"I realized I was hiding," he clarified. "I'd already realized I wanted to send the care package."

"But I hadn't said! That I wanted you to love me."

He crossed his arms and gazed at her sternly. "I didn't feel like I needed your permission." Then his face softened and he smoothed her hair off her forehead and kissed her nose. "I was planning to love you whether you wanted me to or not."

"Huh," she said thoughtfully. "So—you don't want me to tell you, extensively, just exactly how much I want you to love me, and specifically, how?"

"Oh," he murmured, smoothing the tip of his tongue along the seam of her lips, then pulling back to let her see his eyes. "No, I wouldn't say that. I wouldn't say that at all. Do your worst."

And she did.

EPILOGUE

"Is this seat taken?"

Nate stood over her, smiling.

He plopped to the grass without being invited, set his plate down, and took her mouth possessively.

"I love picnics," he said, grinning at her.

"Me, too."

It was their first R&R picnic, and, even more importantly, their first Mira and Jake picnic since the one where they'd met. Alia was blissfully aware of having come full circle.

"Kiss me again," she whispered.

"We're going to get kicked out."

"I don't care." She tilted her face up, her lips parting of their own volition.

"Get a room!"

That was Jake, who dropped to the ground on Nate's other side, followed immediately by Mira.

"We *have* a room," Nate said, smiling broadly.

They did, one they shared, in the staff quarters. Almost a year had passed since Nate had first found his way to R&R.

Nate was now in charge of aquatic programs at the retreat, including all the boating. It was a not-quite full-time job, which left him plenty of time to study for his degree in non-profit management. His long-term goal was to support at-risk youth, steering them towards work, college, and the military instead of gangs and other dead-end behavior.

"We were just reminiscing," Nate told Jake. "You know we met at your picnic, right?"

A strange expression passed over Jake's face. He shot a look at Mira, who raised her eyebrows. "You going to tell them, or should I?"

"Tell us what?" Nate demanded.

"We might have bet on you guys getting together," Jake confessed.

Mira gave her husband a dark look. "*I* bet on you getting together. Jake didn't think you would. But I knew." She smiled warmly at Alia, and Alia smiled back. She had come to love Mira as she'd gotten to know her better this year.

"Hey," Jake said. "I was very supportive, once it became clear I was wrong."

Alia laughed. "He was. And I appreciate it more than I could possibly say." She clapped her boss on the back, and he grinned at her.

She took a moment to survey the picnic. The food table contained many, many delights, including Mira's potato salad and Suzy's homemade cookies. Suzy and Jim were here, at Nate's invitation, standing slightly apart from the crowd and watching with faces that held equal parts joy, curiosity, and sadness.

Alia knew it was probably hard for them to be around so many soldiers who'd survived their deployments, when J.J.

hadn't, but they were doing their best to enjoy themselves. And things were going well for them back home. A new Walmart up the street had only increased traffic to the ever-thriving hardware store, though Jim sometimes griped, on the occasions when Nate and Alia visited them and scarfed up Suzy's home cooking, that there were *too many strangers* coming into the store these days.

Alia secretly suspected he was full of it, that he loved the new faces and their endless questions and crazy projects. Jim had even started a whole arts-and-crafts section to cater to parents and little kids, and though he groused about the kids and their complicated needs, Alia was pretty sure he loved them the most of all his customers.

Mira and Jake's fifteen-year-old son, Sam, had taken Braden under his wing, and they were tossing a football. After a while, Jim drifted over and joined in, and the next time Alia looked up, Jim was all-out beaming. When she looked over at Suzy, she saw that the older woman's face reflected her husband's joy.

A big male body settled in the grass near Alia's feet. It was Nate's friend and former squadmate, Hunter, home between deployments. Hunter was a tall-dark-and-handsome guy with a stubble-stained jaw and broad shoulders—a guy who'd be as comfortable in gray pinstripes on Wall Street as in camo in a trench. "Hope I'm not interrupting."

"Hope you don't mind that I'm about to give you the third degree about Trina," Nate countered.

Hunter had come to the party with his daughter, his daughter's best friend, and his daughter's best friend's *very* pretty mom.

"So," Nate said. "Trina. Just a *friend*, huh?"

Hunter shrugged. "Yeah."

Nate raised both eyebrows, and Alia felt hers follow. "Sure," Nate said. "You just brought your daughter's best friend's mom to a party as a chaperone."

"No, seriously. It's not like that. You know me. I won't go there again."

Hunter's wife had died a couple of years ago and because that relationship had gone south, Hunter didn't ever want to do "serious" again.

Nate gave him a stern look. "You can lie to yourself all you want, man, but life is short. I learned it myself this year. You gotta grab the bull by the balls or the horns or whatever the expression is."

Hunter rolled his eyes. "Thanks for the life advice."

Trina approached and settled herself beside Hunter. Alia smiled at Trina. "So you and—your daughter is Phoebe—?"

Trina nodded.

"—are going to have Clara live with you next year while Hunter is deployed? That's really unbelievably super nice of you guys."

"Clara's like a sister to Phoebe," Trina said, smiling warmly at Alia. "They're total besties. It's one of those things where it's easier having both of them than just one of them, because they keep each other happy."

Hunter's eyes hadn't left Trina's face since she'd sat down. Whatever he said... well, it was clear the man *was* lying to himself. It would be interesting to see what the next year brought.

Across the expanse of grass, Alia caught sight of a splash of blond—Becca. She was chatting with Griff. The two of them had become friends recently, since Becca came down so frequently to hang out with Alia. Becca laughed at something Griff said, and Alia tilted her head to one side. *Huh.* Interesting.

"Hey, guys, excuse me," she said, and rose to her feet as Becca walked away from Griff.

She crossed to her sister. "See anything you like?" she teased.

"Griff's just a friend. He's not my type."

Alia raised her eyebrows.

"He's *not*. Besides, he's still in love with his ex-wife."

"Who told you that?"

"Nate."

That didn't surprise Alia. Nate had adopted his older brother role with a vengeance, and warning Becca off Griff fit the part perfectly.

"I'm going to grab another drink," Becca said. "You want anything?"

"No, thanks," Alia said, and gave her sister a big hug. If she had one regret, it was that moving to R&R had meant seeing Becca less. She watched her sister cross to the drinks table and sent her a silent, secret message. *Know how amazing you are, beautiful girl.*

"Hey," a voice said in Alia's ear, deep and familiar.

"Hey yourself." She leaned against Nate, resting her head on his broad chest, sighing as he slipped his fingers between hers. It felt good, him solid behind her, backing her up, when she was tired and grumpy—and when she was ready to celebrate. In the last year, she'd learned so much about the man he was—always there for her at her worst and best moments, and all the ones in between, but also instinctively knowing when she needed space. In the beginning it would have been difficult for her to imagine that she could love him more than she already did, or that working so hard together at R&R would be just as fun and exhilarating as falling head over heels in love—but it had proven to be true.

"Quite a party," Nate said dryly.

She smiled up at him. He looked back down at her with an expression she knew well. "Dragging on too long for your tastes, huh?"

"Maybe," he murmured against her ear.

The soft shift of his breath over her skin had its intended effect, and she leaned toward him, then caught herself and put a little more space between them. This was, after all, a family show.

"Later." The word touched the curve of her ear and made her shiver.

"Promise?" she asked coyly.

He moved closer to her, let her feel how solidly she could count on his promise.

"Oh yeah," he said, and when she tipped her face up to look at his, his eyes were full of that dark intent. "It's our first picnic as a couple. Pretty sure that means it has a happy ending."

ACKNOWLEDGMENTS

Some books require a little—or a lot—more TLC than others, and this was one of them. Which means the people who saved my sanity get extra lovin' this time around. Huge thank-yous to:

All my beloved Bells, but especially Avery, who told me before I wrote the rough draft that I had the heroine wrong. Bird, next time I'll listen the first time!

Sarah and Jesse Rieth, my patient and wonderful consultants on army matters. Any and all errors, as well as imaginative flights of fancy and deliberate deviations from reality, are mine and mine alone.

Readers Amber Belldene, Lauren Layne, and Audra North, for figuring out how to translate my "I know something isn't quite working but I'm not sure what it is . . ." into great revision advice.

Cheryl Cain, for the breakthrough conversation, in which, among other things, she reassured me that the parts really did fit together.

Mauri Stott, one of my most steadfast and loving critique partners, who had the wisdom to see the story hiding under the story and the honesty to tell me it wasn't on the page yet.

Darya Swingle, for the problem-solving walk and for jollying me out of my book-induced moodiness.

Emily Sylvan Kim, my agent at Prospect Agency, who somehow always has time for brainstorming, and who saw what was best in the book; and the rest of the Prospect team.

Sue Grimshaw at Penguin Random House Loveswept, who edited the first edition of this book. This one was a doozy and she was always kind and gracious.

Charli Teglia, for bearing with me every step of the way. And I do mean every step. If you see her, give her chocolate and take her on a nice walk.

Because this book is a re-release, I also have quite a few additional people to thank, people who have been instrumental in helping me get this book back out in the world (and/or in saving my sanity in the process): Karen Booth, Sarina Bowen, Cheryl Cain, Kate Davies, Christine D'Abo (with sugar and post-its on top), Gretchen Douma, Nicole French, Rachel Grant (again and again), Molly Hays, Gwen Hayes, Gwen Hernandez, Sierra Hill, Christy Hovland, Kris Kennedy, Claire Kingsley, Jaycee Lee, Melissa McCulloch, Kathy McGowan, Alexa Rowan, Ellen Schroer, Jessica Scott (again), Lauren Seilnacht, Sierra Simone, Darya Swingle, Skye Warren, the attendees of Seattle Unconference 2018, the members of Emerald City Author Chicks, the members of Living the Dream Mastermind, and about a bajillion other people. I hope I'm not forgetting anyone, but I might be, because there are so, so many generous authors out there willing to buoy each other up, and everyone I turned to during this process gave their time and support generously.

Also, extra thanks to the best (and sexiest) tech consultant ever, the inimitable Mr. Bell.

ALSO BY SERENA BELL

Returning Home

Hold On Tight

Can't Hold Back

To Have and to Hold

Holding Out

Tierney Bay

So Close

So True

So Good (2021)

So Right (2022)

Sexy Single Dads

Do Over

Head Over Heels

Sleepover

New York Glitz

Still So Hot!

Hot & Bothered

Standalone

Turn Up the Heat

ABOUT THE AUTHOR

USA Today bestselling author Serena Bell writes contemporary romance with heat, heart, and humor. A former journalist, Serena has always believed that everyone has an amazing story to tell if you listen carefully, and you can often find her scribbling in her tiny garret office, mainlining chocolate and bringing to life the tales in her head.

Serena's books have earned many honors, including an RT Reviewers' Choice Award, Apple Books Best Book of the Month, and Amazon Best Book of the Year for Romance.

When not writing, Serena loves to spend time with her college-sweetheart husband and two hilarious kiddos—all of whom are incredibly tolerant not just of Serena's imaginary friends but also of how often she changes her hobbies and how passionately she embraces the new ones. These days, it's stand-up paddle boarding, board-gaming, meditation, and long walks with good friends.